NOT A RAPIST

HEMANT KUMAR

NOT A RAPIST

Novel by

HEMANT KUMAR

Co-Author

RAJENDER KUMAR

Published By

Anybook

Cell : 9971698930

E-mail : contactanybook@gmail.com

Website : www.anybook.org

Price in India : 175/- INR

First published by Anybook in 2021

Copyright © 2021 Anybook

Copyright Text © 2021 Hemant Kumar

Printed and bound in India

Cover Design & Typesetting by Anybook

ISBN : 978-93-86619-76-1

Dedication
to all my readers

Disclaimer

This is a work of fiction. The characters, places , organisations and events described in this book are either a work of author's imagination or have been used fictitiously. Any resemblance to people, living or dead , places, events, casts , communities or organisations is purely coincidental .

Extra-Shots & Thoughts

A big thanks to all the readers for choosing "Not a Rapist" as your read. I feel myself very fortunate, that I got able to present you my story through this book, and I would like to thank each one of them who helped me, to craft this book.

First of all I would like to thank my mother Mrs. Saroj Devi, from her blessings I got the inspiration to read and write books.

I would also like to thank my dear wife Sneha, Who helped me to refresh through her strong ginger tea during the long writing sessions. My little sister Sangeeta, my dear friend Ashok Sirvi who always read my stories with patience and gave honest feedbacks, love you so much guys, and also I thanked to my dad Mr. Rajesh Kumar, my younger brother Lokesh, my cousin sister Sarita and my whole family for their best support.

I would also like to thank Mr. Mayank Sehra for reading the initial drafts and giving his valuable feedback. Special thanks to all my Twitter, Facebook, Instagram and other social media friends, your love and encouragement means a lot to me.

Lastly, I thank you to Rajender Kumar for his valuable thoughts on the story and co-writing this book with me.

"Not a Rapist" is my first book, since my childhood I have a dream to become a writer, this book is a result of that ambition.

Every character of this book is very close to my heart, that's why

I have chosen a character for myself as well.

This is a story about; sacrifice, courage, family, friendship and love.

I do hope that you will like and enjoy reading this book, still after so many hardships there might be some shortcomings left in it, requesting your forgiveness for the same in advance. I will be delighted to have your valuable comments and feedback.

Thanks.

WELCOME YOU TO "NOT A RAPIST"........

May 2018.

Since my childhood days, there has been some characters and places which has kept roaming in my mind, characters which I love the most, characters which I cannot forget and places where I had lived early days of my life.

A long time ago, while returning to my village from Delhi, there was a massive traffic jam on NH-8, it has been raining heavily since morning, that's why I choose some other road to reach my village, it was a short cut route on which I have spent my childhood, and I have made countless journeys on this road. Later on the journey when I passed from the front of my school, some very old memories flashed in my mind. In past thirteen years the building of my school has been changed a lot but still there are so many moments of my childhood which are still as fresh as they were at that time.

Today also when I saw the Kalu's tea stall on the way, my heart felt the same joy which I used to get in my childhood, I stopped my car beside the road and just kept on gazing at the shop as I didn't have the mood to sit alone and have my cup of tea, my eyes got moist thinking about the old happy days of my life.

Today this journey and rain have reminded me about a promise, which I had made with my friend Dushyant, that one day I will write down the story of these moments, characters and our friendship in to a book.

After spending a while, I moved towards my destination, rain was also stopped when I reached at my home. After a little rest I went out of my home to roam around my old hangout places; old Hanuman temple, pond of my village and my fields, everything looks exactly the same as they were in the past, only we people have grown up and changed with the time.

Two days have passed in roaming around and refreshing my old memories, now finally I have decided to write down the story which is tickling in my mind from a long time, I want people to know about this unusual story of love, sacrifice and friendship.

Next morning, I took my laptop and started writing the story from the beginning.

CONTENTS

Chapter 1
Primary Love

I have been restless for many years, Should I tell this story to the world or let those characters remain untold in the realm of my heart. The characters, who made their identity like a lotus in the swamp of the society. In our lives, there are always some people around us who keep alive the feeling of love, courage, and dignity. Those are the people who bring change in the system through their examples. Today I am feeling blessed to share this story of love with you all, in which I have also played a small role.

Dushyant Kumar My best friend, my classmate. He is a diehard fan of Kumar Sanu, he remembered most of his songs orally and he sang them melodiously. In cricket, a fast bowler and hard-core Chai lover. Dushyant lives just 1.5 kilometres away from my home in Qutub Pur, though people from all communities and religions live there still, that place was majorly dominated by Thakur and Yadav communites. His great-grandfather Thakur Kartar Singh was a freedom fighter, and he had worked as the Sarpanch of the village for 15 long years. His son Pratap Singh is the current Sarpanch of the village and Dushyant is his only son. Because of their leadership pedigree, they have a good hold in neighbouring villages, and his family is respected by all. Dushyant and I have played together, studied together, and grown-up together as best friends.

At that time state government was planning to build new toilets around the village but it was never executed and remained as plan only. We also used to go to the farms for dumping and we accompany each other in almost every sort of work. People use to quote or friendship in our village e.g. Jai and Viru of Sholay movie.Metric results were out, Dushyant has got top rank in the school and I also got 2nd position in he got just 2% extra marks from me, it hurts me for 2 days and after that, it became normal as usual. After a discussion with my father, I decided to take math and science in the 11th class. Dushyant has already decided on the same stream. We got admission to VMSS public school which was just 5 km away from my village.

1st July 2005.

Our first day in our new school. There was little greenery around the school and a lot of flower pots placed inside the school which is making the atmosphere serene and positive. Though our classroom was not that big, but it was sufficient for 32 students of our stream. Most of the students are known to us as all of them are from the same or nearby villages. Math and Physics were not as easy as expected, so to counter that we have joined the Excellence coaching center in the market. Every day after school, both of us go to attend our tuition from 3:00 pm to 5:00 pm, where our school teacher Shambhu Yadav teaches us the same maths and physics subject but with a little delicacy and in a different tone as compare to the school. Gradually we are getting our hold on maths and physics. Though we have scored an 80% plus in metric, but we both had been backbenchers since our class fourth, it gave us a different kind of kick altogether.

15th July 2005

We always leave from our school a little late usually as we stay busy in daily chit-chats. That day, it suddenly started raining heavily, and we got stuck at our school. I suggested to Dushyant that we must wait and let the rain stops. But he smiled, and just grabbed my hand,

and pulled me out to the courtyard. Both of us got wet in less than a minute. Then we took our bicycles and started peddling. Initially, I got irritated on his behaviourbut later I started to enjoy the rain and splashes on the road. Though it is difficult to ride a bicycle in rain, but we both are experienced and careless enough to do such things. We are singing songs and riding our bicycles at a high speed on the road. After covering some distance chain of my bicycle got dislocated. As they say "Speak of the Devil," I cursed Dushyant on this and said "I told you Dushyant don't ride too fast else my bicycle chain, might get, dislocate" and look it happened. We stopped on the left side of the road, and I started to fix the chain. Besides us under the shelter of a sweet shop some students are gathered to avoid getting wet in the rain. Dushyant went under shelter too because, Kumar Sanu's *"Sanson Ki Zaroorat Ho Jaise, Zindagi Ke Liye"* song was playing on the shop owner's radio. While dripping off the rainwater from his hairs Dushyant saw a new girl among the other students, who is so adorable that he just cannot take away his eyes from her. Everybody was trying to avoid the rains, but she was feeling the coldness of drops of water on her hands. Her smiling face, that song, and that smell of the soil which is coming from just freshly rained earth. It created a moment of hypnotism for him. He was so lost in the moment that he couldn't hear my voice, I called him twice Dushyant! Dushyant! Let's go, brother, I have relocated the chain on the bicycle, but all in vain. Finally, I went to him and shook my hand in front of his face, and asked O hello!brother are you okay? Let's go home. On this, he hesitatingly said yes. Yes, let's go.

Meanwhile, rain also got slow to drizzling only and students and other people were started to move on their ways. That pretty girl also moved ahead with two of her friends. Dushyant was constantly gazing at that girl while moving towards his bicycle, I interrupted him with my voice again and said let's move quickly as after some time we have to come back for tuition as well. No reply! Finally, I went to him and asked why you are gazing that girl so much? He asked a question to answer my query and pointed his finger towards her and asked who is she? We have never seen her in school or around. I said we are backbenchers bro who always comes late and checks out late too from the school. How can we see normal punctual students? And by the way, why don't you just go and ask her? He told brother you please go and ask about her, please. On this I baffled on him, why would I go? You saw her. You are keen to know about her then you should go and ask her. He insisted again, and I again refused to show interest in it. He further insisted politely, Please go, bro, I will give a treat of Chai & Samosa every day for one week at Kalu's Tea Stall. Though I was not in a mood to go and enquire about that girl but for the sake of Samosa & Chai I can do any task. Ho Jayega! Consider it done, I said you would get full bio-data of that girl by evening. He smiled and hugged me. I went after her, and he left for his home. I closely followed her girls' group and found that one out of three girls is an acquaintance to me, named Payal. She stopped after a while and that pretty girl moved ahead shaking her hand as a goodbye to her. I interrupted her Hi! Payal, Hello she said, long time no see. Then I just formally chit-chatted with her and after a few minutes, I directly came to the point. By the way, who's that girl? I haven't seen her here before. Who that tall one? She pointed towards one of them. No, the other one that girl with a pretty smile. Oh, that girl, she is with us only in our primary school, how could you don't know about her. I was surprised to know that. After a few minutes of discussion, I Thanked Payal and bid goodbye to her. I was so happy inside, as I got all the vital information about her and I felt a sense of achievement in this. After all, it's about the seven days Chai & Samosa treat.

At six O'clock we reached to Kalu's Tea stall. Now tell what info did you get? Asked Dushyant. Slow down man I said let's sit first, No! Man first tell me about her! Have you got her name? Relax brother just sit, He was so curious to hear about her, as I was excited for my 10th result once.

"Kavya," I said. Her name is Kavya. How sweet! He said. Hot Samosa's and Chai arrived on our table. I just took a Samosa to eat, but it couldn't reach to my mouth. He stopped my hand in between and said first tell me every tiny detail that you got about her. Man, she's Kavita. She is our classmate from primary school. Who Kavita? Asked Dushyant. I said that girl with two ponytails and red ribbons, our Kavi! Remember? After some moments he recalls Oh Kavi! No, it's not possible Kavi was not like her. She is our Kavi bro, I said. But she has changed a lot, she looks very pretty now and how could she get her admission to VMSS? How does Kavita become Kavya? Dushyant asked. I said she went to Kota for her studies with her maternal aunt. Where her aunt changed her name to Kavya in high school as Kavita is quite old fashioned, which was named after her grandmother Kavita Devi. She became studious there and scored a distinction in 10th standard and the rest of the change in appearance has usually happened when someone moved to the city from a village.

Oh, I See! But then how come she doesn't recognize us? That I don't know bro now please let me eat my Samosa, as it's already cold and I moved my focus on Samosa & Chai, but he was still thinking about Kavi only. After the tea also, he was constantly talking about her only. We got late that day in our discussions, and my mom scolded me badly for coming home late. Later on the bed, I was wondering that how Dushyant will sleep tonight.

Kavita for everyone but Kavi for me and Dushyant, she took us

6 years back to the memories of our primary school. December was a bit extra cold in the year 1999, we used to eat peanuts and Gazzak in the afternoon. Though I used to get up early in the morning with my mother to feed our cows but I have made a rule for me to bath on alternate days only. Half-yearly exams were in progress, but due to the lesser availability of rooms, students form two, or sometimes three different classes used to be merged for examination. It was our paper of maths Dushyant was sitting on the bench on my right side and at my front desk, there was a studious looking girl was sitting. Suddenly she turned back to me and said "Bhaiyya" do you have an eraser?

I got annoyed on calling me a"Bhaiyya" and though I have the eraser, but I denied her straight forward. Abruptly Dushyant interrupted in between us and said I have one you can take mine. After using the eraser, she gave it back to him. At this Dushyant was blushing towards me, and afterward also his complete focus was in the girl only instead of his exam. That situation continued in the coming three exams also, she always forgot the eraser and Dushyant use to give it to her. Then he just keeps blushing and looking at her throughout the examination. He got attracted to her, she also responds to him with her sweet smiles. That is the beginning of a sweet love story in class fourth, the first love of their life.

Kavi uses to bring peanuts for me daily so that I can forget her "Bhiayya" remarks as soon as possible. Now all three of us are good friends, but the feelings of Dushayant for Kaviwas more than a friendship. Kavi also feels the same way for Dushyant. Our trio uses to hang around the school every day. We all are having a great time together, but that time was running so fast. We all have cleared the fifth standard and we are looking for admission in the 6th standard to a new school as our primary school was up to the fifth standard only. Dushyant got 3rd position in the school and I also scored good marks but Kavi has scored only 55% marks due to some medical issues during her final term. She was upset about this. We couldn't ask her as to which school she is getting enrolled as summer break is already commenced.

Dushyant and I used to meet as often as possible and we used to discuss things about Kavi. But we didn't know the actual location of her home. She used to join us from the main road's Yadav sweets shop. Both of us were a little upset about this and one day we have decided that we will search and find her home. The next day we went to that road from where she used to join us for the school. After a few minutes of a walk an enquiry, we came to know, that the isolated house in the fields was her home. The joy of finding her home was visible in our eyes. Finally, we are going to meet her after a long time. At the entrance of his home, we saw a young boy (*around 16 years) we interrupted him. Hello, brother, do Kavita lives here, is she is available at home? No! He replied and asked who are you and what do you want from Kavita? I asked him who you are, by the way, she is my sister he replied. Oh! We are in the same class so we just want to meet her. For what he asked? I said she had one of my book with her, and we are here for that only. On this he replied that she wasn't in the town now, she has gone to her aunty's place. Where? Dushyant asked. That's none of your business he replied irritatingly. (I thought it was better to leave now, as we know her home and we can come later also to meet her.) It's fine we can collect that book later and we left from there. Both of us are sad that day as we couldn't meet her.

Few days have passed but it seems like an era has gone, but then I got a little hope from my mother's word about the forthcoming fair of Hanuman Mela. This skit comes in several years only when it happens to be a full moon night on June month's Tuesday. It's customary here in my village and all nearby villages to visit the fair and pay a visit to that ancient banyan tree temple of Lord Hanuman and take his blessings. It was famous there that whoever visits the temple during the skit, Lord Hanuman will surely fulfil all his or her wishes. During the skit, everybody including the people who are not in town also pays a must-visit at the temple. This is one of the biggest and most popular fairs around the town, it has a lot of colours, foods, swings, toys, and music in it. I got so excited about this news, and I rushed to Dushyant's home on a hot afternoon of June on my bicycle. Sweating and panting heavily I reached to him, what happened bro? You're here in this hot noon? He asked me surprisingly.

My dear bro! There will be a skit on coming Tuesday in the village andI have a firm belief that Kavi will definitely visit that fair. My mother told me that people of all seven villages from our council might be out of town, but during this skit, they will visit the fair for Lord Hanuman's blessings.

Yes! Dadu also told me about the fair, and he bought a new pair of Kurta Pajama for me and himself. (Surprisingly) But I was oblivious that Kavi might come to the skit, then he hugged me and asked let's have Coca-Cola on this. We went to a nearby shop for the cold drinks and cheered our bottles and said. "Jai Bajrang Bali".

On Tuesday, there was a lot of hustle-bustle in the village all around. Everybody was in a rush to reach the temple today. Food stalls, toys, and other stalls have already settled on Monday evening a day before the skit. One big red colour hammock was placed first time in the fair and kids were so excited to swing it that. I have never witnessed such big vibes ever before for this event. I also bought a new Kurta for myself of sky blue colour matching to Dushyant's Kurta. Dushyant and I went to the fair ahead of our parents. Usually, we use to go there for holy food only but this time, we first went to Lord Hanuman's temple and offered our prayers. With closed eyes and folded hands in front of Lord Hanuman, both of us prayed to have a glimpse of Kavi today and somebody pressed the bell of the temple. It seemed to us like the Lord Hanuman has listened to our prayer and there was a smile on our face now.

Gradually, a large number of people started gathering in the fairground. Devotional songs of Lord Hanuman were playing on the loudspeakers. Our parents also joined the skit, and they told us not to do any escapade around and reach back home timely in the evening. They also gave us 20 Rupees each, for sweets and to have a joy ride in that large red swing. Everybody was so happy and positive around the fair. But our eyes are just looking for our friend Kavi only. It's been mid-afternoon since we are waiting for her, I don't know about Dushyant but the smell of the delicious holy food from the temple was distracting me a big time. We are wandering here and there for her but I felt like that smell is calling me towards itself as I was famished.

Now it's three o'clock in the afternoon and I bring some holy food to eat and we ate our lunch sitting in the shed of that old banyan tree. The tree was on a decent height, the whole entrance of the fair was visible from there. People are coming there into groups some in large and some in small groups. Few people are coming on a tractor-trolley with loudspeakers on them, while some are coming on camel carts. But still, there was no sign of Kavi.

In the evening there was a big wrestling match was also organized by the fair committee and a large crowd was gathered to see that fight. We just walk all around the circle of the fighting ring, looking for Kavi. Two tall bulky wrestlers are fighting with each other inside the ring, and people are cheering loud on their moves. The wrestler from Qutubpur has won this match but we are losing our hopes to see Kavi today. And then in the evening we just sat quite sad, near the big red hammock. There are mesmerizing tube lights all around that hammock, but we are quietly watching that swing. Dushyant was looking very sad and disappointed and to cheer him up I asked him to let's take swing on the Hammock. He resisted initially, but I forced him to join, just to cheer him up. We got boarded on the hammock, and the operator locked our box and swing started to move up. There were butterflies in my stomach while reaching up at the top and coming down to the ground. It started moving slowly in a circle. Fresh and clean air was flowing and there was a lot of noise of music around. Finally, we got some relief from the scorching heat of the summer, and cool air refreshed us a bit. Suddenly I saw a girl in the white suit moving back her red printed stall from his shoulder, and my heart skipped a beat it was Kavi. I pointed my finger towards her, showing Dushyant that she is there. But our swing started to move at a faster speed now. She was moving towards the parking with her brother and other family members. Dushyant shouted loudly Kavi! But his voice got lost in the noise of skit. He even tried to get off the running hammock, but I stopped him to do so. She was moving away from us, in front of our eyes, but we just couldn't do anything. After a few minutes, she just got in the vehicle and moved out of the fair parking. When the hammock stopped Dushyant de-boarded quickly and ran towards the parking but she was gone too far. We got very disappointed on this, I recall and cursed myself that why we prayed for her glimpse only? If we had wished for a meeting with her, Lord Hanuman would give us that too. We sadly returned to our home late at night and both got scolded for this from our parents.

Two months of summer break was finally over, and we both got our admission in Adarsh Govt. School which was quite near to our home. For the next few days, we use to go to her home every evening so that she might come out and we could see her. Three weeks have gone, but there was no clue of Kavi. Dushyant got affected on this but after two months life gets back to normal. Rarely a few times her name came in between our conversations, Now Dushyant also moved on from her. With time we have learned the hard part to live without her.

This was the fourth standard love of Dushyant, which he has lost somewhere.

Chapter 2
A Rival

Perhaps this is one of the happiest days of Dushyant's life. He is going to meet his first love which he had lost a few years back without a proper goodbye. Will Kavya recognize him? Or she has forgotten all her memories with him. Let's see what will happen next.

Dushyant woke up early today and got ready too early than usual, out of excitement to meeting Kavya. I met him on our meeting point for the school, he yelled a little I am waiting here since half an hour where the hell have you been. Relax! Bro I said I am on time, perhaps your watch is running fast today. Anyway let's go now, and we got on our way to school.

After ages, we reach to school before the time and our eyes are looking for Kavya only. After a while, we found her in the courtyard giggling with her friends. Dushyant's hearts skipped a beat on this, and he got completely lost on gazing her face. Indeed, she was looking so adorable at that time that even I thought for a moment that Kaash! He didn't address me as Bhaiyya that day then I would have given her that eraser and we would have been together now. Alas! Anyway now she is just a friend and girlfriend of my best friend Dushyant.

Dushyant lost his focus on her with the sound of Morning Prayer's bell. Kavya and her friends went towards the assembly ground for the prayer. While crossing the path from us, Dushyant called her name, Kavya! She turned back towards us and asked Yes! Hi, how are you? Dushyant asked. I am fine but who are you? Kavya replied surprisingly. Of course, how could you recognize me after a gap of 6 long years, even I couldn't get you right in my first look.

Look how much you have changed, but that change is for good only I must say that. Excuse me! Who are you? Do I even know you? Kavya Said. Yes, we know each other you please guess who I am. On this, she got little irate and moved ahead saying please excuse me, I got to go for the prayer. She started moving towards the assembly, Kavi Dushyant called her from the back. She stopped on hearing this name, I am your Dushyant. She turned back and gazed his face curiously, a tear from her left eye drops out then from the other eye also. Are you mine Dushyant? Asked Kavya. Yes, I am Dushyant and he is Hemant. Hearing our names, she smiled a little and walked towards us. Dushyant was also in tears. He walked towards her and holds both her hands and hugged her. Both are crying but with tears of joy. They have not uttered a single word and just kept hugging each other tightly. Other students were shocked to see this kind of behaviour in the school. To avoid any trouble, I interrupted them. Hello! Sohni Mahiwal of Rajasthan let's move the ground before our PTI teacher come to us and punish us. Well, we all smiled and moved towards the prayer ground. I saw little flashes of the past when we three used to go the prayer like this. I was so happy inside for both of them.

She was in arts streams. 11th C was her class, and we asked her to meet after school. Both of us are waiting outside the school at the ice cream stall. She came out with her friend Payal and one other girl, and after seeing us she bids goodbye to them and walked towards us with a smile on her face. She was just crossing the road, then Atul interrupted her and said Hi! Kavya how are you? Shall I drop you somewhere? While accelerating his bike. (Atul, a genius of mathematics and brilliant cricket player of the school. Though he rides Hero Honda Splendor, but he doesn't consider himself less than Shahrukh Khan.) Hi! She said, not today Atul my friends are waiting for me and Thanks for asking. Bye, she said to him and walks towards us. Dushyant and I started looking at Atul like an enemy at that moment. Hi! She said to us, and we both started walking holding our bicycles with her.

Dushyant: Kavya why did you left us without saying a word, we have searched you for many days and even we went to your home also. We met your brother he told us that you left the town.

Kavya: Yes, there was no goodbye, but inside I knew it, that we will defiantly meet back soon.

But at least you should have informed us that you are leaving the town, I asked her with a low heart.

Kavya: Actually! I went to my maternal uncle and did my studies till matric there. My maternal grandmother was not keeping well those days. My maternal grandfather was also too old and my only uncle uses to travel out of the city often because of his business. So I helped my grandparents there, but yes I use to miss you guys every day.

Dushyant: We also missed you so much Kavi but you have changed a lot now. You look so pretty now. Kavya blushed on this and thanked him for the compliment.

Kavya: both of you have changed a lot also. I just can't recognize you as well.

Although the sun was a little bit scorching, but we couldn't feel it because of her soothing eyes. And we walked towards home talking and giggling about our old days.

After a while, Dushyant asked her why you chose arts over commerce and science.

Kavya: I want to become a lawyer one day, a big lawyer and I will fight for the justice of innocent people. What about you? You wanted to become a cricketer like Zaheer Khan.

Dushyant: Yes! Cricket is my passion but my dad wants me to become an engineer.

What about you Hemant? Asked Kavya. And we moved on reliving our old memories. Now going to school together is become our daily routine. Life has become a 70MM Bollywood movie for us which has everything in it joy, laugh, friendship, and love. But every love story has some villains in it, Atul and his friends were not so happy with our closeness with Kavya.

One day Kavya left for home a little early, that's why I and Dushyant went straight to Kalu's tea stall. We are about to reach the stall suddenly Atul and his loafer friends crossed our way with their bikes and stopped us in between. They are wearing sports uniforms and carrying their cricket bats and wicket stumps along with them. I got a little shocked on this but Dushyant was so firm.

Atul: Hey you both I didn't like you people roam with Kavya around. She is an innocent girl. You both just stay away from her. I like her and she will be my girlfriend in the future.

Excuse Me! Dushyant said.

Atul: Treat this as a soft warning!Otherwise you people will drag yourself into a big trouble.

Dushyant went forward and looked straight into the eyes of Atul with anger. I stepped up and came in between both of them. I said, I know she's beautiful and any boy will fall in love with her. But why do you want to become Salman Khan of Saajan? But Dushyant pushed me a little aside and said what you are barking dog.

Dushyant: Kavya is my childhood friend and don't you ever dare to take her name with such disrespect otherwise I will change the geography of your face. I am warning you guys, keep this thing clear in your mind and head.And a punch came from my left, bats, stumps, kicks and smacks. It became a fight club within a few minutes then Kalu's tea stall staff and customers split us to stop the fight. They are five people and we are just two, but we gave them a good fight. We got some bruises but as they say, everything is fair in love and war.

News of this spat reached our home before us. Seeing the bruises on my face and hand, my dad took my cricket bat and hits a pull shot on my bump. I screamed Ah! Thank god, my mom came in between, she got emotional seeing blood on my face and saved me from dad. To know what happened with Dushyant it took me four days, as I was not able to walk because of the strain in my leg, post that fight.

Atul and his loafer friends bashed us badly in front of Kavya's brother and presented the wrong facts about us. He already remembers us from the time we went to his home and enquire about her. Atul told his brother that we follow Kavya on the way from school to home, we bother her during the school also. Overall Atul created our image as roadside Romeo's in front of her brother. He scolded Kavya badly in front of her parents and asked to stay away from us.

Afraid of her brother Kavya created a space form us, now she rarely uses to meet us. And whenever we try to meet her, she always acts in a hurry and talk so less. She lives in fear, that somebody might see her with us and tell his brother about it. She has changed her timings and always accompanies her friends so that we cannot approach her.

Dushyant's father was also so angry with him. It was so disgraceful for their family that how come a real Thakur's lad got bruises in a street fight. His uncle threatens to kill Atul and his friends. But his grandfather stopped him saying their intervention in child's fight will neither be appropriate and nor appreciated as well. His family was not on a talking term on this act of fight, but he was sadder because of Kavya's ignorance. He got off the track from studies also, he was so upset that he just can't be focused on cricket studies or tuition.

I was also concerned for him, not because of his separation with Kavya but I was assuming the danger of a big bloody fight again soon. And this time mom will not able to save me from dad. Our happy reunion again became a big mess and its hurting Dushyant more than the first time.

Time was running so fast that our exams came on the board, the first time I scored 23% extra marks from Dushyant in 11th standard. But I was not feeling any happiness about it, as his focus was completely not there in the studies. I was so concerned about him.

CHAPTER 3
PULL SHOT

It's been a week since we have electricity in our village, in this super-hot summer in the month of May our only electricity transformer at the intersection of our village caught fire. After so many attempts of my Dad and Sarpanch Ji, we finally got electricity in our village, but time and again there will be malfunctions in that transformer due to fluctuations in voltage. In the night we all are sweating because of the humid, suddenly we saw light in our bulb and fan started moving, there was a loud cheer in the village on this.

13th May 2006.

I am so happy today, it looks like a festival in my home and why not, after all we have got our new telephone connection today through Rajasthan rural telephone services "Rainbow". It was the first telephone, in our vicinity, I am feeling go so proud of this. My dearest Mom did first call to her father in Jaipur and my father called his brother and exchanged our contact number with them. My family was so happy about this new white telephone, now they don't have to stand in the queue of PCO telephone booth. My Mom also made Kheer (Indian traditional dessert) that day. Then I gotmy turn to use it, I called up Dushyant. Her mother picked up the phone, I greeted her aunty Namaste! And asked for her wellbeing. She knew me very well as I have visited her home often. She called Dushayant loudly and said it's your friend's call please come and speak to him.

Dushyant: Hello, Who is speaking?

Hemant: Now you even don't recognize my voice on the phone?

Dushyant: No, it's not like that bro, tell me how you are? And form where are you calling?

Hemant: I am fine bro, I am calling from my home. You just note down my new telephone number. That's great!he said. After a few minutes of talk, I told him to let's meet tomorrow at the playground for the semi-final match.

"Yuva Cricket Club Alwar" uses to organize an inter-village cricket tournament annually, it's a fifteen over match series which is useto played with a tennis ball.

No! He said I will not be able to play tomorrow as I have some strain in my leg. I know you very well brother and I know you're lying to me now. Please do come and play for your village, your team needs you. Tomorrows match is with those Rampur guys, and Atul is the captain of that team. This is the best time to take a revenge from him on the field. Dushyant was paused on this, I said I will wait for you tomorrow on the ground and I hung up the phone.

Next-Day Morning.

Atul was famous for his battinglike "Sehwag" in all villages. He played a magnificent inning and scored 74 runs in just 52 balls. With his powerful batting performance team Rampur have scored 143/3 in fifteen overs against team Qutub Pur. Dushyant was not at all in his usual line and length today, he bowled a very bad spell today. Out of vengeance, he was just kept trying for bouncers against Atul, that's why he has given 15 extra runs through wide's and no balls only. In his spell of four overs, with five sixes from Atul and 15 extras, he has given 60 runs with zero wickets. Qutub Pur crowd had a lot of hope from him but it all gone in vain after his performance.

Dushyant was the only player who can still turn back this match to winning side. I tried to connect with him during the innings break, but he was so upset about his performance that he has requested me, we will talk after the match.

Second innings.

Dushyant Thakur took the strike along with Kapil from his team. His team and Qutub Pur crowd were expecting a big opening partnership from them. On the Bowling side, Charan Singh the strike bowler of Rampur took a long run-up and made some changes in the field. Atul Yadav was fielding atthe point encouraging his team through claps and cheering them with "Come on Boy!"Slogan.

Dushyant was ready on the stumps, Umpire signals Charan to start the ball. Charan started with a beamer, beating Dushyant, ball goes straight to the hands of wicketkeeper. Charan Singh is a very fast and skilled bowler of Rampur. Yesterday also, he took a Hat trick against Biranwas village. Once again Charan bowled from the same end this time Dushyant played a cut shot and ball goes for the boundary beating Atul at the point for four runs. Loud cheers in the crowd, Dushyant and Qutub Pur opened their accounts with a four runs.

Dushyant and Kapil batted sensibly and managed to score 33 runs in 4 overs without loss of a wicket. Atul was pushing his bowlers so hard to get a wicket,andbreak this partnership. He changed the fast bowlers with the spinner Salman, and he got the wicket of Kapil caught behind the stumps on the very first ball. After that, no batsman was able to stick on the batting crease though Dushyant was standing tall on the other side on 85 not out. Dushyant played so well and stretched the game to the gate of victory, now Qutub Pur needed only

3 runs from the last 4 balls but it was the last wicket partnership on the ground. Atul was burning in agony and bashing his teammates to get his wicket. Charan was on the bowling side he delivered a full toss, Dushyant pulled it on the leg side and calls for 2 runs but excellent piece of fielding by Salman in the deep, he restricted them to a single only. Now 2 runs needed from 3 balls for a win and 1 run to draw the match. Dushyant went between the crease and asked Bunty to just play the ball softly and run for a single. On the other side Atul went to bowler end and said, this is our chance Charan we need get this last wicket, we have to win this match at any cost. He does some changes the field and bring players closer to the crease, to stop the single. Charan took a long run-up and bowled a speedy Yorker and he clean bowled Bunty. Dushyant bend on his knees on the crease and Atul started cheering madly in front of him. It was sheer bad luck for Dushyant and his team thatthey just lost a winning match.

Out of exhilaration and arrogance, Atul came to Dushyant and said just like this match I will clinch Kavya from your life, you motherfucker. He laughed louder and teased him badly chanting "Looser, looser"repeatedly. Out of anguish Dushyant raises his bat in the air and knocked off his head. A big layer of blood started falling from the right side of his head and he fell on the ground. There was chaos on the ground, people were ruining here and there. I and members of Yuva Cricket club rushed to them. Charan took Atul to the nearest hospital on his bike. He got a severe injury on his head and got twelve stitches. Somebody informed the police as well. Atul's family members and some local villagers reached to Dushyant's house.

Thakur Pratap Singh, father of Dushyant was beating him badly and cursing him for his deed, while his grandfather was watching all this sitting on his chair and smoking his Hookah. His mom was somehow trying to convince his father to stop beating him, saying please stop now it's enough, after allhe is a child. Though, it was a very tense situation at his home but it was looking like a typical Bollywood scene to me. Atul's Parents and Police reached inside his house, Sub-inspector greeted his grandfather, Namaste Thakur Saab, and he welcomed everyone inside.

Kartar Singh Ji, your son is the Sarpanch of this village and your family is one of the most respected ones here, but that doesn't give a license to your grandson to keep fighting with people time and again, said atul's father.

Yadav Ji, I am so regretful about what he has done with your son. Inspector please take him with you and follow the due course of action. He has spoiled the goodwill of our family and village, said his father. Atul's Father to Thakur Saab, we and all nearby villages respect you a lot and they give an example of you and your family,but your grandson has attacked on my son the second time and this time he got 12 stitches on his head and the injury was so severe that he might have lost his life this time. But fortunately, he is alive.

Thakur Saab: Yadav Ji, your village is just next to us and we are like old neighbours, we have been together in our joys and sorrows. Dushyant isa young boy and has hot blood, you also know today's youngsters. But because of these child fights, we must not create any rivalry between our villages. Atul is also like one of my children. We will bear all the cost of his medication and medical expenditures.

Gulshan Yadav (Atul's Father): Thakur Saab, My father was a friend of yours and he fought with you for our country's independence. My whole village respects a lot your family and just because of our past relations I am not filing any official complaint about this incident but I request you to please make understand your grandson, not to disgrace the glorious heritage of your family.

Inspector: This time I am letting go of this case out of your respect but if such thing happened next time, then out of obligation I have to do a proper police inquiry. Anyway, I will take leave for now Namaste!

After everyone left, Thakur Saab called Dushyant to sit with him. He asked him, I can see at your face that you're restless now a day, you kept so busy in yourself that neither have youtime for me nor you prepare my Hookah now a days. I missing our little chit-chat with you, like we used to do earlier. My dear son, if you have any kind of problem, you can share it with me without any hesitation. After all I am not only your grandfather, but we are friends too my son. Thakur family has a great reputation in nearby villages, please don't spoil our family's name out of anger, son. I have a lot of hope in you that you will take our family's reputation to new glories in the future. Remember one thing,your grandfather is always there with you no matter whatsoever,now come let's have dinner with me.

Summer holidays of school comes to an end, but in these 2 months I hardly had any words with Dushyant. I have tried his telephone several times but he refused to talk with anyone. Just one day before the commencement of our school, finally I got his call. I felt so happy on hearing his voice after 2 months, he asked me to let's meet tomorrow. I called up Kavya also to meet tomorrow. I was so excited to meet my friends tomorrow at the school.

It was our first day in a new class, I started a little early from the home but Dushyant was already waiting for me at our meeting point. We both smiled from far after seeing each other, and we hugged. Tears of separation spreads out of our eyes. Enough man let's go to school else we would be late for our school he said smilingly. We got our bicycles and walked towards school and after a few minutes, we saw Kavya was waiting for us under a tree. There was a little smile on her face which was so contagious that we also had the same blush on our face. On this, I thought to hug her tightly but at that time handshake with the girl was in trend, and hugging a girl was not accepted by people. But surprisingly Dushyant moved forward and hugged her, Kavya pushed me also in. That day that tree and that group hug is still so fresh in my memory today as well.

Finally! Our good old days are back, we often used to visit Kaalu's tea stall to have Chai and Samosa but sometimes we have cold drinks only. Dushyant is also back in his old form in studies. Everything was going so smoothly, we all have happiness around us.

November has just started and it was cold outside. We both are coming back from our tuition and we have a plan for Chai and Samosa at Kalu's tea stall. The moment we reached the tea stall, from far I saw Atul and his friends are already sitting there. Seeing this, I asked Dushyant let's go home I don't have a mood of having a Chai, we will come tomorrow. Dushyant also saw them and he understands why I am avoiding it today. He said No! bro, we will have it today only. We got inside and he ordered two special cups of Chai. On this, Atul teased him saying yes Kalu bring special Chai as he has nothing special in his life apart from your Chai, and his friends laughed on this. Dushyant moved up a little to answer those bastards but I grabbed his hand and stopped him. Please, bro just ignore those crap guys. He somehow controlled himself and sat down.

Atul: stood up and said attentionmy dear friends, everybody gazed at him. I have to make an announcement, the reason of today's treat. I have a new sweet girl in my life and we just become friends in summer holidays only. Congratulations! Man everybody cheered to him and toasted their cold drinks bottles. Tell us more about her, one of his friend asked him. She used to meet me every evening near the pond. She has soft cheeks and she walks like a peacock. She looks so hot in her tight-fitting Kurti's, and her name. Please tell her name man, we are dying to know about that beautiful chick, his friends asked him with a mischievous laugh.

Her name starts with letter K, KA..V.. Kavya, her name is Kavya and a loud laugh among his friends. She is so hot man, congratulations dude, his friends started wishing him.

Dushyant got mad on this, and he rushed to punch that bastard. I stopped him forcefully in between and said he is lying bro, he is just instigating you. On this Atul and his friends started a louder laugh. Atul with fierce eyes came close to his face and said, Dude, see I love Kareena Kapoor so much and I can't help it, though she doesn't love me, that's a different story, similarly you don't have the status to love Kavya, you can only dream for her but you will never get her in your whole life. Kavya will never love a loser like you, but she has a very soft corner for me in her heart, Because I am the champ of the school man Still, if you have any doubt about my words then go and ask my Juliet that I am her Romeo. HAHAHAHA

These words of Atul acted as fuel added to the fire, he got mad after listening all this crap. Your cups of Chai sir, our order arrives on our table. Out of anger Dushyant just broke the cups on the ground. Calm down you looser, better you have shown this attitude on the filed in the game. Somehow he controlled his anger and went towards his bicycle. I followed him, saying calm down bro, he is just instigating you. We left from there but Atul and his friends kept laughing at us loudly.

If you have not stopped me today, I would have broken his head again, He yelled at me. I will see that bastard in the future. Brother that's his trick to make you angry so that you take some wrong step again. He just wants to instigate you so that you do something wrong and your parents permanently stop you meeting with Kavya. Only few months have left in our 12th board exams than all three of us will join some good college in the city. Just keep a tap on your anger till that time and please focus more on your studies.

After reaching his home Dushyant called me up but I was not at home at that time, later I called him back but he was not at home. So I called up Kavya and asked about him. She said yes she got a call from him and he was sounding a bit upset today, he has asked me to meet him tomorrow. I felt bad that he has asked to meet her only and not invited me to join them. Maybe he has called me for that purpose only, I was so concerned for him.

The next day Kavya was waiting for him post the school near our meeting point under that banyan tree. Dushyant is also gone to meet her alone, he reached there and said Hi to her. She was trying to hide her face in her scarf. Dushyant understands that she is hesitating a bit to meet him alone, after all the past incidents. They both went to the mango tree and sat down under its shadow.

So what's that important thing that you want to discuss with me? Kavya asked him.

Dushyant: Nothing much of importance as such, it's just that I want to meet you in person.

Kavya: but why personally, we usually meet every day in school and where is best friend Veeru?

Dushyant: He's busy with some work at home.

Kavya: Okay, so how's your preparation going on for the half-yearly exams?

Dushyant: On track so far.

He is hesitating today while talking to her and Kavya recognizes it that he wants to say something important to her. Maybe she knows it already, what Dushyant is about to speak. Dushyant wants to express his feelings of love for her, but he just can't do it.

Listen, Kavya breaks the silence, I want to discuss something with you. Oh, please say it, Dushyant said.

Kavya: I want youto control your anger, Time and again you're arguing with Atul and his friends. They all are loafers and they instigate people intentionally just for fun. I don't like those guys at all, as they use to stare me like anything on the way to school.

Dushyant: I will screw those Bastards! (Angrily).

Kavya: See! That's why I don't want to tell this thing to you, now you will definitely get in a spat with those for no reason.

Dushyant: No reason? How can I be quiet if anybody is teasing you?

Kavya: Oh really? Tell me what you will do with them.

Dushyant: I will twitch them if anybody will stare you with bad eyes.

Kavya: Oh Really! But why?

Dushyant: Because you're my friend, a special one!

Kavya blushes a little on hearing that special word from him. Dushyant also started blushing out of joy. The whole scene is looking like that song of Kumar Sanu. "Do Dil Mil Rahe Hein, Magar Chupke Chupke."

Dushyant: Okay, tell me what you like? I mean do you like

traveling or any place you like to visit?

Kavya: Me? Though I didn't think about it but yes I like lakes and hills a lot. I would love to visit a place which has a lot of lakes. I will go and sit beside the lake to watch the sunsets every day. I had made my mind that whenever I will feel like I have everything in life or I want nothing from life then I will move into Udaipur the city of lakes, I heard a lot about it that is a beautiful place to spend your life.

Dushyant: Indeed! Udaipur is a very beautiful city and it has so many lakes. I have visited there and roamed around Fateh Sagar Lake it was a wonderful experience for me.

Kavya: I will defiantly go there one day.

That was a memorable evening for them, though he lost his golden opportunity to express his love to her, he enjoyed her company a lot. They are laughing and discussing small little joyful things about their lives and aspirations. But there's always a night ahead of every evening. Before Kavya reached her home her brother Randhir got the information about their little date through one of Atul's informer friends. Kavya got a big lecture from his brother to stay away from that Thakur lad. Friendship with him is too far, you don't even talk to him now onwards. Her parents also guided her to keep her focus on studies only. His brother falls in Atul's trap and asked him to be watchful, on her daily activities.

For the next few days, Dushyant tried a lot to have a word with Kavya, over the phone, in the school, and after that as well but all goes in vain as he didn't get the right opportunity. That day I felt the pain and helplessness of a true lover,whocannot express his feelings to his beloved. This might be because hedon't have the courage to hear a No from his beloved. Some people just can't live with a rejection, that's why they choose to live a life of a one-sided lover.

November has passed on a sad note for Dushyant and half-yearly exam of 12th class is about to commence in December.

Our first exam of English was scheduled on 10th December. Finally, Kavya asked me to meet her after school at Kalu's tea stall to discuss about the exams. Chilly winds are flowing from the east, and Kavya sipped her Chai with shivering lips. She was holding the cup of Chai with both of her hands to take some heat from it. She was looking so adorable that day. Dushyant was gazing on her from the past few minutes with so much love that he might get up and hold her in his arms at any moment. He was even not blinking his eyes, He was so much absorbed in gazing at her. Iinterrupted him saying your Chai is getting cold bro please have it first, and later you can carry on in your important work. He got a little embarrassed on this and some giggles floats between us.

After that day Dushyant becomes so desperate to win her love for him. Every morning while going to school he just gazed at her silently. Kavya was also getting prettier every day that was an effect of winters or it's because of his love for her. I have heard this from someone that people get prettier when they fall in love or when someone starts loving them. Now I have a firm belief that those saying are true. Her innocence made Dushyant fall madly in love with her.

On 16th December it was our exam of physics, Kavya doesn't have an exam that day as she has the Arts stream. While returning from the school, he asked me, listen bro can you do me a favor? Of course Thakur Saab you just order it, I said it in a teasing way.

Dushyant: I know you have a hobby to write, and you also want to be a writer in the future. Can you please write something for me? You know what I feel for Kavya, but I just can't express it, in front of her. I don't have the courage to tell my feeling for her, Can you please write my thoughts in a letter? Will you do this little favour for me?

Oh my goodness! It seems to me like a 90's Bollywood movie's love story. Bro, I will love to write your letter and one day I will surely write a book on your love story.

Dushyant: Write to her that since our fourth standard in school I have a big crush on her. The day I don't see her it feels incomplete to me, her presence makes me feel complete. Though I tried several times to tell her how much I feel for her, but I just can't. He kept on telling his feelings, and I started to note it down. I will give you the final letter tomorrow, said Hemant.

Dear Kavya,

"Kavi" My hearts need to recite this name every day for my heartbeats. Whenever I think about my childhood, I can't remember much, but your pretty face appears rystal clear to me, as it was just like yesterday. I am thankful to you that you forgot your eraser that day, which paved the beginning for our friendship. Do you remember those Gazzaks that we ate in the cold winter afternoons and those cold drinks which we had together in summers? Those are the best moments of my childhood, Thanks Kavi for making my childhood a memorable one.

I got shattered when you left me without a proper goodbye, but by the grace of goddess Maa Bhawani, we met again. For others you are Kavya but for me, you will always remain my childhood friend "Kavi" the poet of my life. Often I felt to tell you what I feel for you, you're much more than a friend to me. But I couldn't tell you that's why I am writing this letter to you with opening my heart in it.I don't know whether I am right or wrong but all I know is that I can't live without you now. Whenever I don't see you for a day, I felt some kind of anxiety around me, Aloo Ke Paranthe, Kumar Sanu songs, and Kalu's Chai all looks tasteless to me. Whenever you smile Kavi, I just can't take away my eyes from you, I just want to keep gazing you for hours and do nothing. Now I want you to call me yours and you please be mine forever.

Meeting you was fate, becoming your friend was a choice but falling in love with you I had no control over. Your love for me has never needed an expression from your end.

A look in your eyes is enough to make me realize what you feel for me. And if you have the same feelings for me, then just kiss this letter in front of me tomorrow.

Yours only.

Dushyant.

The next day, Dushyant gave that letter to Kavya and asked to read it in free time. Kavya read this letter on reaching home. Dushyant couldn't sleep the whole night, in the wait of her reply. The whole night he kept thinking that how Kavya will react to his letter if she got offended on this then and so many other things.

The next day Kavya met us after school, but she was so calm like nothing happened. There was no expression of joy or sorrow on her face. On the other side, Dushyant was so restless to know her answer. We tried to have few words with her, but there was no discussion about that letter. Dushyant thought that she might got offended by his letter. We are so confused and tense at that moment. After a few minutes, Kavya's stopped on her turn for home but out of tension, we both walked forward without saying a good-bye to her,we moved a few steps ahead only, and she called us from the back hey listen! She showed that letter to Dushyant and kissed it. Dushyant jumped up out of joy and she walked towards her home smilingly. Dushyant hugged me so tight and kissed on my cheeks, passing by travellers might be thinking that we are gay. I haven't seen my friend so happy and expressive in my whole life. Inside me, I also felt happy in their happiness. I prayed that moment to the God, now no bad eyes of others, affect our happiness.

CHAPTER 4
CRIMINAL WINTER

There is famous saying here in India that "New love bird's chirps a lot" and it was clearly visible in their life too. Dushyant and Kavya use to have long conversations over the phone, even they had long talks at night too. They do not realize about the time when they talk to each other. Even on the way to school, they just pass smiles to each other for no reason.

We got a slight relief from the studies, as half-yearly exams were finally ended today on 23rdDecember 2006. Winter season break will begin from tomorrow, so to celebrate our last day of the exam and commencement of our winter vacation we all went to Kalu's tea shop. I was enjoying my Chai and Samosa as there will be no school from tomorrow, but Dushyant seems lost somewhere. He was thinking about how he will meet Kavya as school will remain closed for the next 8 days.

Two days have passed of our winter break, but I didn't get any call from Dushyant, even I tried his phone twice but no luck as he was not available at home both the time. I often tried his phone at night also but it was always busy. Seven Days have passed, but I didn't have a single word with him, Only 3 days have been left in New Year and there was a vibe of joy in the cold winds of December, but I don't know why my heart is a bit restless these days.

On the other side, Dushyant was dying to meet Kavya from last 6 days. Every day he insists Kavya to meet him somewhere near by her home by giving some excuse to her family, But Kavya was helpless as after those past incidents her parents were strict on her stepping out of home and his brother is already watchful on her through his spies Atul and his gang.

Recently Dushyant's parents bought a new VCD player for their home, and he got so addicted to it that every day he watch a new movie at home. During these days there was a rage of Hollywood's 18+ movies in our village, and our youth was so addicted to this. Dushyant also use to bring some adult VCD's at home to watch as it was a new experience for him. At this stage of age youths easily got influenced by such addictions and maybe this is the reason that he was having very less time for me as well.

29th December 2006

On the northeast end of our village, there was a huge farm of Kavya's father. Now a day he is harvesting the crop of wheat. He starts his day early in the morning by giving water to his harvest, then he keptoccupied whole day in the field. He does a lot of hard work like every other Indian farmer. Kavya's brother Randhir was assigned to deliver food at the time of lunchand Chai in the evening to his father on the farm. He also helps his father in some other works related to harvesting in the field. It was Friday today and Randhir has to go to a nearby city Rewari due to some work of his father. So after providing the lunch, he went for Rewari and assigned Kavya to deliver the Chai to father in the evening. Around 3:30 pm her mother initiated the process of Chai making, and Kavya called up Dushyant.

He picked up the phone and said "Hello".

Kavya: Oh my dear, where are you today?

Dushyant: Just look around yourself, I am always close to you heart.

Kavya: (She smiled on this) and asked can you come and meet me today?

Dushyant: Of course! Just tell me when and where?

Kavya: Around 4:00 pm in the evening, near the Oak tree at the corner of our farm, I will wait for you there, but I have a scope of 15 minutes only, Request you please come on time as I don't want to waste any single moment of those 15 minutes.

Dushyant: O my darling! I will be there before half an hour as I am dying to see your pretty face.

He just hang up the phone and got dressed in his new red puma t-shirt and went straight to the meeting point. He reached there much priorfrom the scheduled time and he started waiting eagerly for his beloved.

Winter season was at its peak, and Dushyant was also on a blue moon as he is going to meet his beloved after a gap. It was yellow all over the fields the colour of mustard flowers is floating allaround. He was thinking in his mind that he will hug Kavya and hold her for 15 minutes.

Kavya is looking so cute and adorable in that Sky blue Kurti and Dushyant felt that she has the most beautiful girl in his life, and top of it her silver bangles in her left hand, 2 stubborn swirl braid which fleeing on her face, gracefully covering her shoulder with her stall and those intoxicating eyes with black mascara are instigating him to lose his control today. He was so indulged in gazing at her that he just forgot everything for a minute.

Knock Knock! She just waved her hand in front of his face. Are you there? Kavya

Asked him. Oh, Yes, how are you, my dear? He asked Kavya.

Kavya: Feeling much better now,after seeing post a long gap.

Listen! I have limited time I have to provide this tea to my father will you accompany me?

Dushyant: What about Randhir, your brother? He must be there on your farms.

Kavya: No he is not there, only Papa will be there.

Oh Okay! Let's go, but I need some time of yours, I want to discuss something important with you.

Kavya: No please not now, otherwise Chai will get cold.

Dushyant: Just five minutes, please! I will keep it short, I promise you, please!

Kavya was silent on this, which he took as a yes. Then he grabbed her hand, and they walked on a narrow footpath of the field to an isolated place near the tube well. He sat so closed to her and kept a hold on her hand throughout, both are gazing at each other with blinking their eyes. The evening was a bit cloudy that day and soothing fresh winds are floating from the east. On top of that, the sound of flowing water from the tube well was creating a romantic atmosphere around. All these things together and those two love birds, it was indeed a mesmerizing view for anyone. Kavya's heart was beating very fast, she was afraid that somebody might see them together then it will be a big issue for them. After taking some hold on her breaths she asked him "Now tell me what you want to discuss."

Dushyant: I can't tell you like this, I feel shy in front of your eyes. Please close them for a moment.

Kavya smiled on this and closed her deep eyes like a sea, perhaps she also wanted to feel the moment now instead of the mere seeing each other. Dushyant came closer to her. He is already holding her one arm in his hand, and he placed his other hand on her face gently. He moved his hand through her hairs, to her cheeks and to her neck. Her heart was beating so fast that anyone sitting close to her can hear it. Dushyant further moved closer to her face and placed his lips over her lips. She gets rid of her hand from him and placed them over his neck and pushed him closer to her. They are completely lost herself in that moment. They are kissing each other so passionately and that romantic atmosphere was adding more joy in their kissing. Dushyant felt that he was in some Hollywood movie scene right now as he was so much influenced by those movies now a days. He didn't even realize when his hand reached to her breasts in between, Kavya Shook his hand from there, but he was so engrossed in kissing her that he tried to press them again, Kavya shook his hand more firmly this time but he kept trying for this forcefully. Kavya got angry on this and she just backed off him, she stood up, and started leaving from that place, but Dushyant's senses were not in control, he has completely lost his mind, He grabbed her wrist forcefully, bangles of her hand got shattered, and drop of blood spreads all over her Kurti. He has thrown her on the ground and he inserted one of his hand under her Kurti and started pressing her boobs forcibly. Kavya started crying on this, tears were following out of her eyes. Dushyant breathing heavily said, nothing will happen Kavya trust me I love you, you just enjoy the moment. She was trying full force of her body to get rid of him, but he was uncontrollable for her. In all this scramble, the kettle of Chai spill down and spread all over her sky blue Kurti and mascara of her eyes also spreads badly on her face, she has lost all her charm and she looks scared now, She kept on begging that please stop Dushyant I don't want this now, for God's sake please stop this. He was looking unstoppable and further his hand went down to her panty.

BACHAO! Kavya screamed very loud on this, SOMEBODY,

PLEASE HELP ME!

Hearing her scream, some nearby farming neighbour rushed towards her, and they separated Dushyant from Kavya and grabbed him like a beast. Kavya got up and covered her torn clothes with her Dupatta. Herfather also reached there, Kavya rushed and hugged him crying. Her father consoled her, with his hands, and before he could ask anything he saw towards the noise where the crowd is beating Dushyant badly.

After few minutes of hustle, Atul's and his gang member also came and joined the crowd in beating Dushyant. His face has become a poster of bruises, blood, and marks, there was blood all around his legs, mouth and hands. Someone informed her brother Randhir too, who was just returning home from Rewari.

He just arrived on the spot and he was so angry at that moment that his eyes become so red, like they are filled of acid, He screamed Mother Fucker! And just dragged him on the ground, he kicked his face with full force and a splash of blood came out of his mouth. One of Atul's gang member gave an axe in Randhir's hand,he was breathing so heavily, that he could have killed Dushyant at that time, if Kavya's uncle Karan Singh Yadav have not stopped him, He stopped Randhir and took the axe away from his hands. His uncle gets closer to Dushyant, to recognize him,isn't it that same guy, that Thakur's lad?Whosliced the head of that Rampur guy? Again Randhir grabbed the axe and rushed towards him, screaming step aside uncle, I will kill that bastard today. Stop it! Have you gone mad? There's no benefit in killing that bastard, take him to the village in front of everyone, Let every member of his family suffer for his heinous act, and I will make sure he will live rest of his life in hell. Atul smiled mischievously on hearing this.

Kavya's father has three brothers and he is the eldest one among them. Her youngest uncle works for the Police department,this means that Dushyant's life is going to become a hell for sure.

People say that news of bad incidents spreads like fire in the jungle, within few hours this was the breaking news of the town that "Thakur's lad have raped Yadav's daughter in the fields."

At that time I was listening "Dhoom Machale" song on my FM radio, suddenly I heard ladies of the town whispering to each other that, One Qutubpur boy had raped a girl in the field. I lowered the volume of the radio and asked my mother, what happened? Who did what? Nothing happened, you go inside and do your studies, she said. I came inside and switched off the radio and called at Dushyant's home phone number to know about the news but it kept on ringing nobody answered it. I don't know why but my heart got a bit restless on this, I was feeling a little suffocated, so I went up to my terrace, their peacocks are screaming loud. I recalled that my grandmother uses to say that "Whenever peacock screams in the evening that will bring some bad news to the people" I got scared of this. I was feeling so low now, So many questions are running through my mind. Then a boy from next to my house came to my terrace from his terrace and said; "did you know? Your friend has committed a scandal, He fucked that Yadav's chick in the field."

WHAT! For a moment I felt that I have lost ground under my feet, my body got a tremble and my lips started shivering, I spoke slowly, fucked her, Means Dushyant, Did.. NO! No! this cannot be true. I rushed downstairs on my wooden ladder with my trembling feet, my mom scolded me be careful and come down calmly else you might get hurt. Why are you in a hustle, she asked me? Mom I have to rush to my friend at Qutubpur, everybody was saying that my friend, done, with Kavya. Mom that boy Atul, definitely he must have done something wrong and blamed my friend Dushyant. Mom you please come with me or tell dad to join me else those people will kill my friend. I was panting heavily, and I can't firmly remember what all I said to my mother. She got scared hearing this and pushed me forcefully inside the room,then she started interrogating me who's this Kavya? How do you know her? Tell me truth,you will not step out of your room, I will go and call your father right now, you have my swear, don't step out of this room until I come back with your father. She locked me up in my room and went to see my father.

"My mother knows Dushyant very well, but she doesn't know about Kavya and she was not aware of the rivalry of Atul and his gang as well." After a few minutes she came back with my father, and she might have told my father the whole story on the way. He opened the door and slapped me so hard that I got a print of his hand on my face. Don't you dare to step out of this room else I will break your legs and he left the room out of full of anger. I can understand the reason for their harsh behaviour,my parents are concerned about me,and they don't want that I get into any trouble with this police case and all, even I was also so scared.

On the other side, Qutubpur village has a silence like a graveyard. Everybody was inside their home only,it looks like the same scene of Bollywood movie "Sholay" when the villain Gabbar attacked the village.

The moment when Thakur Kartar Singh heard about this news, he got fainted and fell on the floor. At this stage of his age, he was not able to sustain this kind of news, it seemed like a nuclear attack on his family,some people rushed to check Dushyant and some stayed with Thakur Saab at home.

Many years back, there was a big combat happens between Qutubpur's Thakur and Yadav's Dhani Yadav because of fields boundary line. Massive blood bath happened in that fight and in this same clash Kavya's uncle, Karan Singh Yadav has got a deep wound on his left leg and he got crippled, that wound was given to him by Thakur Tez Singh, Dushyant's Uncle who alsowas mysteriously drown in a river and died, after a few months of that clash, From that day onwards Yadav's and Thakur's have a strong feeling of revenge in their hearts.

Today's incident have fuelled and reignited that cold fire again. Dushyant's cousin took Thakur Saab and rushed to the hospital and here his father Thakur Pratap Singh and mother reached on the spot. His mother started crying madly on seeing her son lying on the ground, there was mud and blood spots were all over his body. But till now Kavya's youngest uncle, Basant Singh has moved his pawn ahead in the game, he is bragging his power of Policemen in his uniform. Dushyant was lying unconscious on the floor, and he dragged him up to police van. Hearing her mother's weeping voice he got a little sense and out of pain, he called his mother "Maa" in a very low voice. On this her mother begged with folded hands to the policemen, "please leave my child I beg you, he cannot do any crime, he is innocent please leave my child." Police van moved from there and she falls on her knees, Dushyant's father consoled her and took her up. Atul's gang and other people standing around started taunting them.

Kavya and her family also went with his Uncle Karan Singh for a medical examination separately.

Dushyant's father and his Uncle along with few fellow villagers reached the police station, while few other females and male villagers took his mother back to their home. Thakur Kartar Singh rushed to the police station directly after getting his conscious back in the hospital. The atmosphere of the police station was so negative and surely was not in favour of Dushyant. Everybody was so concerned and numb about this unexpected tragedy, they have no idea what to do now and from whom they can seek help.

Kartar Singh asked duty officers, where is my grandson? Please let me meet him once.

Policeman: Sarpanch Ji, He is not here right now,they have taken him to Alwar, where he will go through testing and all.

What kind of test? His father asked the policeman.

Policeman: (angrily) UPSC test! Don't you know what scandal your son have done? You can go and check it in the Alwar police station.

Kartar Singh: My grandson cannot do any such act, somebody is trying to trap him.

Policeman: Thakur Saab, I respect you a lot, but please don't try to spoil that all. Whatever you think about your grandson, you must quote it in the court now, I can't help you anything in this case now.

Dushyant's cousin speaks to his grandfather, Sub-inspector Basant has already bashed about Dushyant now there is no benefit staying there, we must move to Alwar police station. That very moment all men of Thakur family reached Alwar but they were not able to meet him,they spent the whole night traveling here and there, and waiting inside the police station.

Next day, early morning before the case reached to judicial court, local newspapers have already declared Dushyant a Rapist in their newspaper headlines;

"BREAKING NEWS! Sarpanch's Son raped aminor."

"Qutubpur Sarpanch Thakur Pratap Singh's only son Dushyant, age 18 years, brutally raped a Yadav's minor girl in the fields and tried to kill her afterward, Police have caught the convict on the spot, and further investigation is in progress."

Thakur Saab got a big shock after reading this news, all his respect and legacy have gone for a toss in a single day. In Alwar also, nobody heard the helplessness of the Thakur family, they just kept running from the police station to the collector's office throughout the day. Thakur family was in despair and highly demotivated now. On the other side, his mother is weeping throughout the day and even didn't have any food from last night. After two days with the help of a crime branch senior official of Rajasthan police, local authorities allowed Thakur Saab to meet his grandson.

Policeman: Are you the father of that rapist?

Thakur Kartar Singh: No! Sir, I am his grandfather. He cannot do such a heinous crime. He must be trapped in this. (With folded hands he begged the policeman.) Please release my child sir, he is innocent.

Policeman: Your grandson has done rape with a minor girl, tomorrow he will be presented in the district court, have you hired any lawyer for him?

Thakur Saab: Lawyer? For what sir? It's an issue of our villages and as per our tradition, we will deal with this matter in Panchayat, our village arbitrage. Sir, our villages don't believe in this court case and other legal technicalities.

Policeman: Your grandson is charged under section 375 for rape and section 307 for attempt murder by Yadav family, after two days he has his case date in district court, I suggest you to hire a good lawyer ASAP, otherwise whatever is your wish.

Thakur Saab: But sir… "Policeman interrupted in between".

Policeman: You have 5 minutes to see your grandson go and meet him, I have other important works to do.

He pointed other fellow policeman to get him to the Dushyant's lock-up room and left from there.

Finally, after 2 days Thakur Saab saw his grandson, he was lying near the lockup gate. He called him Dushyant! On listening to his name from his Dadu after 2 days, it gave him hope, and he rushed near to the gate.

Dushyant my child, Thakur Saab grabbed his face which was swollen and full of blood and bruises. It hurts Dushyant a little, and he was not able to speak due to his injuries, thirst, hunger, and dark thoughts of his mind. Thakur Saab moved his hand gently over his wounds and some drop of tears dropped from his eyes. He was pleased to meet his grandson after 2 long days, but he was not happy seeing him in such a condition. He controlled his emotions somehow and said "Dushyant my son please don't worry, everything will be fine soon,this is really a bad time for us, and this shall pass soon." The policeman calls Thakur Saab your time is over now let's move out. Yes sir, one moment, please! And he told Dushyant don't worry my child and always remember your grandfather is always there for you. These words gave him the much needed hope and he smiled very mild, Thakur Saab kissed his forehead and left from there.

Thakur Saab came out with moist eyes but with a little satisfaction of seeing Dushyant. He told the whole story to Dushyant's uncle and his father and asked to hire the best lawyer for him to get released his child out of this hell. This was the first time for them to handle a court case and time was also very less. They got under the influence of a crook lawyer and hired him. After taking hefty advance payment from the Thakur family, he assured them that he would try his best to get Dushyant out on bail.

They all reached back at home at night, seeing Thakur Saab head down like this Dushyant's mother started mourning again. She has already read that news in the paper today and she knows their family's respect is matters a lot to Thakur Saab. Nobody had dinner that night as well, his aunt made Chai for everyone and everybody was awake whole night, thinking that how to get Dushyant out of this problem.

The next day, Thakur Saab and his father went to Kavya's home to ask for forgiveness and asked them for a settlement in the village arbitrage only,they also became ready for any kind of penalties they want. But Randhir and his uncle Karan Singh sent them back empty-handed and dishonoured them in front of other local villagers.

New Year 2007 has begun with this life-changing tragedy, there was absolutely no amount of happiness in our lives.

After the government holiday of New Year court opened and the prosecution has begun. But in this battle, Thakur's family already has very few arrows in their quiver. On the other side, Vinod Bagadi the lawyer of Kavya's has made a strong maze of plea's to trap Dushyant. Kavya has been used likea puppet in all this, she was frightened by her family, that she can't able to see the helplessness of Dushyant's mother and sadness of his grandfather. Under the influence of fear and threats of her family, she was not able to help the love of her life.

Dushyant, was screaming in front of court that I am "Not a rapist", I have not done any wrong with Kavya. But Sub-Inspector Basant Singh has produced a false medical report of rape. Both of her uncle and lawyer made a solid case against Dushyant, then how come the judge can go against their plea. Bagadi has read the statement of Kavya in loud voice, on the behalf of her statementthe judge has convicted him for a rape and attempted murder and sentenced him for 10 years of imprisonment with labour in Kishan Garh jail, for his family it was like a home imprisonment for 10 years.

Whole Thakur family was so helpless today, nobody was there to console them. Cheap policemen and colleagues of Basant Singh even not allowed to meet Dushyant to his mother. She kept crying and begging to release his son in front of policemen. His father and uncle kept running here and there in Alwar for few days to reach out for his bail, but law seemed very helpless against this ill-legal plotting of evidence and hostile victim. After wasting a few days finally they returned to Qutubpur with empty-hands and no hope.

Kavya's uncle Karan Singh is a very shrewd person, and he has also warned strongly, Thakur Tez Singh before his mysterious death that he will defiantly take revenge for his crippled leg in the future from Thakur Family.

Here I also paid a huge amount for my friendship with Dushyant, after this incident my parents got me rusticated from VMSS School in between the running term. Studies of 12th class left unfinished in between, later I was sent to one of my relative for some time. There was not a single day when I have not missed Dushyant and Kavya, this whole incident looks like a bad dream for us, I wished some morning I woke up and see this was a bad dream only. I have lost one important year of my schooling and become so silent and sad afterward. My parents are also concerned about me after this change in my behaviour. I tried a lot to be happy and engage myself in studies and other things but I just can't forget about Dushyant and Kavya. This incident has changed me a lot from inside.

Next year my parents got my admission to a government school 15 Kilometre away from my home. Where I completed my studies of 12th standard. I have no connection or news about Dushyant and Kavya now, but I heard that his grandfather Thakur Kartar Singh was not keeping well after that incident.

Chapter 5
Guilt

5 Years later.

Monsoon was at its last stage of the year and "it's raining like cat and dog" since morning here in Jaipur. I took a half-day today from the office due to some headache and went straight to my apartment for rest, I took one pain killer and went straight to my bed, after some time I got awake because of the continuous noise of my phone's ringtone. I look for the time it was nine in the evening and I got 8 missed calls from my mom, I got a sense my mother will screw me up for this and as expected she went on fire,"Why you didn't pick up my phone? I called you several times but no answer even no message as well? You already know that I got concerned for you because of your behaviour, but you don't care at all about yourself and us! That's why I keep forcing you to get married so that some beautiful girl will come and take care of you,now you become a big engineer that's why you don't listen to your mother, earlier as a kid you was very obedient as a son" and she got emotional over the phone. Oh, my melodramatic mom, I got asleep that's why I couldn't take up your phone, Now you please stop crying or else I won't eat dinner tonight, I gave a phony threat to my mother just to stop her from crying. "I am not crying, I am just saying that." Then I got interrupted by a call waiting from an unknown number,but I ignored it and continued my discussion with mom. Again I got a call from the same number, but I ignored it again, on the third attempt, I said goodbye to my mom and picked up the call.

Unknown caller: Hello! Hello is this Hemant?

Hemant: Yes, speaking. (It was a girl's voice which sounded somewhat familiar.)

Unknown caller: Hi! I am Kavya. (I was paused for a moment) Hemant are you there she asked?

Yes, Kavya! I said. (I was shocked to hear her voice after so many years.)

Kavya: How are you?

Hemant: I am good, you say how's life?

Kavya: I am good, okay listen! I need your help! Please don't disappoint me, I got your contact number after great difficulties.

Hemant: My help! In what matter?

Kavya: I am at Gandhi Nagar railway station, Can you please come and pick me up?

Hemant: Gandhi Nagar, what are you doing there at this time?

Kavya: I cannot explain to you everything over the phone, it's raining so badly. Please come fast and pick me up, there are too many people around me and I don't know anyone here in Jaipur.

Hemant: Okay! Just hang on there, I will be there in 20 minutes.

I took the car keys and rushed to the railway station, windshield wiper of my car was moving on top speed as visibility was too low. I was driving the car too fast, but my mind was running even faster than that in the nostalgia of our past lives seven years back. Every memory just becomes alive for me Dushyant, Kavya and my home in my village where I had not been from the past few years. Why Kavya turned up to me after so many years? that question is haunting in my mind like running clock with so many questions along.

It was showing 10:15 pm in the big clock of the station, I parked my car in the parking and rushed to the station exit gate. I called up

Kavya to come in front of the inquiry room, I am waiting there for you. I got a little wet in rain and I was just splashing the rainwater from my wet hair then only I saw one very pretty girl coming towards me from the front, dragging her American tourist trolley on the ground. Her smile is still as contagious as I saw her for the very first time on that rainy day. People say that "Time will turn your good moments back in your life once for sure", for me that was the moment. In blue well-fitted jeans and white Kurti, She was looking much prettier than my childhood friend.

Thunders of clouds and the sound of lightning, before I could have uttered a single word, Kavya comes straight to me and hugged me warmly. I was so confused at that moment, Shell I hug my old childhood friend or fight with her, for what she did with Dushyant and our friendship.

After a minute she breaks the silence, how are you Mr. Engineer?

Hemant: I am fine, tell me about you?

Kavya: Well, it's a long story let's go home and have some Chai first, It's been ages since we had our Chai together.

Hemant: Yes, of course! I helped her with her baggage, and we moved towards the exit gate. I took the car from the parking and pick her from the exit gate. The rain was not in a mood to get stop today and it got heavier than before. There was a frequent sound of lighting in the sky and inside my heart of our scary past but there was a pin drop silence in the car.

After a few minutes,

Kavya: I know what you are thinking, I am the culprit of yours and Dushyant,and I am in deep guilt for what all wrong I did, but now

I will not stop myself to correct the things.

I was still quiet on hearing all this with no reactions.

Listen! I have left my home forever! Kavya Said.

Hemant: What! I pressed the sudden breaks out of shock. Why?

Kavya: Because I love Dushyant, I have done so much evil to my beloved and my friend that god will also not forgive me, and she started crying.

Hemant: Oh Please! (Out of burst) If you have valued the love of my friend, then you would have saved him from going to this Hell, You have ruined our friendship and his life forever.

Kavya: Please give me a chance to explain my helplessness once, I promise if you still feel me a culprit then I will never bother you again.

I was so angry at her for what she did, but I couldn't bear my friend crying in front of me.

After 30 seconds of silence, please stop crying, I consoled her,let's go home first then we will discuss it.

Around eleven o'clock we reached at my apartment, I unlocked the door and asked her to change the cloths, bathroom is there on the left. I went to the kitchen to make Chai for us,while making tea my anger for her calm down and now I saw a little ray of hope. We sat together on the couch, and I served her the Chai.

Kavya: (After sipping the first sip of Chai, she got a little smile on her sad face),it just reminds me of the taste of Kalu's Chai.

Hemant: Did you still remember? Those were the best days of my life,my friends, fields, ambitions and those evening Chai treats at Kalu's shop, what else can someone ask for.

Kavya: Yes, I also miss those days.

Hemant: Now please tell me why you left your home?

Kavya: I want to re-open Dushyant's case file.

Hemant: What! Are you serious?

Kavya: Yes! Now I have a full realization of what blunder I did with my life. It was the biggest mistake of my life for which I cannot forgive myself ever. I cannot go back in time to correct the things, but yes I will get Dushyant out of the jail anyhow. Yes, Dushyant tried to make out with me that day, for which I denied also, but he didn't raped me.

Hemant: WHAT! This means he is suffering because of a false allegation,did you lied against him in the court, did you gave false testimony in the court? WHY? How could you do this to him? He is the love of your life, Dam it!

Kavya: Yes! I know, at that time I was not even aware of what rape is and what can be the consequences for the same act,my brother and uncle threaten to kill me if I don't do as they said to me, they have given me every tiny detail which I need to spoke in my statement. Nobody was ready to listen to my part that I love him, and I called him up there to meet me. We are just sitting with each other talking, later we kissed each other that too he did it with my consent. Later on, he got a little excited and started to go further but I refused for it as I didn't want all this at that time. I was trying to stop him, later some villagers came I between,later, you know what happened. I got scared and terrified, I was under tremendous pressure of my family to spoke against him. From that moment onwards I could not look into my eyes. I am so embarrassed and regretful about that.

Hemant: This Means my friend is suffering in that hell from past 5 years for no criminal offense. (I got shocked), I am getting mad now, and I can't handle this truth. (I took some deep breaths).

Kavya: I am suffering inside for this guilt from last 5 years, but not anymore. I will fight for him and set him free from those cages, Will you be with me in this fight?

Hemant: Me, how?

Kavya: I realized my mistake a few days later when he got convicted, for a false rape. I want to correct my mistake that day only, but I was helpless, but then my ambition to become a lawyer got stronger than ever, I studied so hard and cleared my LLB this year only. Now I can fight for his case in the court,the moment I told my family that I love Dushyant and I will re-open his case, than they all shouted on me like anything. My mother, brother, and father everybody was against it as this will defame all their respect in the village. They threatened me to evict me from their home forever, but I am not that little girl now, I am an adult and nobody can stop me to fight for my love, and set Dushyant free from the jail, That's why I left my home forever.

Hemant: Are you clear in your mind, on what step you have taken against your family and society?

Kavya: These family members and society people are so selfish, they just always think about themselves,they never thought about any individual's feelings and emotions. Now I have decided to raise my voice of truth against them so that this will not happen to some another Kavya, but I need your help in this, Will you stand on my side in this case?

Hemant: Of course! But how,what I have to do for that?

Kavya: Just be with me in this journey, because apart from Dushyant you're the only person with whom I can share my feelings without a second thought.

Hemant: I just want to see my friend free from that cage,from the first day I had a firm belief that he just cannot do such crime, He loved you so much that he didn't utter a single word against your allegations.

Kavya: When did the last time you met him?

Hemant: 24th December 2006.

Kavya: What? (Shockingly).

Hemant: Yes, I just can't face my best friend like this, because I am the one who was not there with him, when he needed me the most. I don't have the courage to face him (shredding a tear from my eyes) I moved my face away from her, as I don't want to show them to Kavya.

Kavya: (Tears dropping from her eyes) so you don't have any news about him in the past few years.

Hemant: No, news as such, I went to meet him twice in past years but he refused to meet anybody,but yes I frequently write letters to him but no luck of a reply back from his side. I don't even know that my letter reaches to him or not.

Anyway, it's quite late at night do you want to eat something? I can order it for you.

No thanks, I already had my dinner on the train,she said.

Let's go to sleep then,you can use my bedroom I will sleep here in the drawing-room, do let me know if you require anything.

And we bids goodnight to each other.

Next morning, on the breakfast table.

These Paranthas are too yummy! From where you learned to cook? She asked.

Hemant: from my mom, she had taught me everything before I shifted here so that I can eat healthy home-cooked food instead of outside unhealthy food.

That's great, she said.

By the way from where you get to know about my phone number? I asked.

Kavya: I got it from Payal.

Hemant: Oh, Okay.

Kavya: You left VMSS School in between, my family also shifted me to Indore to my maternal aunt for higher studies. That was the most difficult time of my life, there was not a single day when I have not missed you guys.

Hemant: I can understand it, as I had been through with same phase in my life.Somehow I managed to clear my 12th class, after that I went to Delhi for further studies. I was trying for AIEEE (All India engineering entrance exam) but cannot scored a good rank in the merit list, finally ended up in RPET (Rajasthan pre-engineering test). I did my B.TECH from RTU (Rajasthan technical university) and got my placement here in BSNL.

I am sorry Kavya, because I am cursing you from past five years for all these miss happenings in our lives as I didn't aware of your part.

Kavya: It's okay, I can understand.

Hemant: So, now what will be the further course of action?

Kavya: I have gone through his case thoroughly and made a file of his complete history and facts. Now on Monday, we will file a petition for his release in Jaipur high court, I have a firm belief that the court will rethink about their decision of his conviction, but it will take some time, as you know all about the speed of government processes, but I will try my best to expedite it.

Hemant: Okay, but what about Randhir and your Uncles?

Kavya: I know they will not sit back and relax, they all are afraid becausethis case can show their real faces to the world. I know that it will give a big blow on my respect in this society, but I can't bear this load further on my head for the injustice I had done with him, He has suffered a lot because of me, now if I can set him free and save his rest 5-year terms of Jail, then I will think as I have done my atonement from this sin.

But before all this processing we must go and meet Dushyant, it's been years since we have seen him.

The next day we went to Kishan Garh jail and requested the jailor to meet Dushyant. Jailor told us that in the past five years he has neither met any outsider,nor he is vocal inside the jail, He is just passing his sentence quietly. You people are wasting your time here, he will not meet you.

I requested him again, sir please pass this message that his friend Hemant has come to meet him from his village Qutbupur. On my persistence, he sent a constable to inform Dushyant about me.

After some time he came back, fortunately, this time he was agreed to meet me, maybe his heart melted to the name of his village. I was so happy to hear that,the jailer was also supersized on his agreement to meet a visitor. I rushed with the constable to meet him, Kavya also started following me but I stopped her and requested to wait for a while,first let me meet him, and afterward you join me,but why? She asked me.

Please try to understand as I don't want him to react, then she agreed to wait.

We have gone to an empty room where Dushyant brought in by a constable,we kept looking at each other for a while with a pin drop silence. He had a beard and long hairs but he was still looking innocent as he has those radiant eyes which are speaking his truth loudly. His curious eyes are looking at me with hope, tears of joy dropped from my eyes, I rushed and hugged him tightly, Dushyant's dry eyes had no more stock of tears to spread out.

Hemant: Please forgive me, brother, I could not do anything for you. I am not worthy of your friendship, I even didn't turn up to meet you for the past 3 years, please forgive me.

And I burst out crying with all my grudges and helplessness of past years. He hugged me more tightly and patted on back.

Dushyant: It's okay! Brother, I can understand your situation, please don't cry now. I have no grudges with you, now after seeing you today, I am feeling relieved and happy as I haven't seen anyone my own, my well-wisher from the past five years. I missed everyone a lot, you, my family and our village.

Hemant: Don't worry Brother, though I have this belief from day one that you cannot do such wrong act any cost, and now I know that you are innocent. Nothing physical happened between you and her,you're trapped in the plan by those vengeance hood people,but now the whole world will know about the truth and justice will prevail.

Dushyant: It's been 5 years, what I will gain now by telling people about my truth. I was proved guilty for the crime that I didn't commit and now these rods of the cages are my destiny, I am scared now by the people outside this jail.

Hemant: No Brother! In that horrific phase of our life, time was against us, but now we are together and we will get you out of this jail. You have your full life ahead, we all love you brother, I, your mother, your dad, Dadu, Kaya everybody.

He interpreted me there after hearing her name.

Dushyant: Kavya? Sigh! After ages, I heard her name in someone else's voice, I wish that she has not made that mistake to ruin our love.

Hemant: Brother she has realization of her mistake, and she is cursing herself from the day of your conviction,but she also has some obligations and complications in her family, that's why she can't help you at that time,but now she wants to re-open your case herself and redeem herself from that sin.

What! He said shockingly.

Hemant: Yes, bro, she has done a lot of hard work to become a lawyer for your redemption,and she want to meet you now.

Dushyant: No, Not again brother I don't have that trust on anyone now.

Hemant: It's not like that brother, she genuinely wants to get you out from here.

Dushyant: But why she wants to do this for me now, why she wants to scratch my old wounds, I don't want to get hurt again,please!

Hemant: I understand she made a big mistake at that time, but she was not mature enough to take a stand for her own decisions,she was under tremendous pressure from his uncle and her family.

Dushyant: And what about my family? What's their fault in all this? She has ruined all our respect and legacy into dust.

Hemant: Listen to me brother!

Meeting time is over, you have to leave now. (Police constable came in and asked me to leave.)

Hemant: Tomorrow I will come again brother, you please think about what I said to you with a fresh mind. Please meet her once, listen what she says, then do whatever you wish.

He was silent on this.

Hemant: Take care brother.

I hugged him and left the room with the police constable.

Kavya was waiting for me outside eagerly,she rushed to me the very moment I came out and asked me for his wellbeing.

Hemant: I am sorry Kavya, He denied meeting you today, but don't worry, I will try to convince him again tomorrow.

She was very said on hearing that, but I gave her the confidence that Dushyant will be ready to meet her soon.

Next morning again we went to meet Dushyant.

In the meeting room.

Hemant: have you given a second thought to what I said yesterday? Kavya also came with me, she is waiting outside. Yesterday also she came to meet you, meet her once at least?

After gazing at my face for some time, he turned his eyes downward in a yes, I requested the constable, a girl is waiting outside the room please call her in, and within a minute she entered the room, in her white suit with tears in her eyes.

Dushyant was still gazing down to the floor, gradually she walks towards him and called him "Dushyant" He didn't move an inch from the chair, but he can't stop his tears, one tear fell on the ground from his eyes without his permission. Kavya hugged him from the back and started crying. I just can't judge her state of mind, whether it was tears of joy of their reunion after that long gap or it's just because of the guilt that she was responsible for his condition.

Kavya: I know you will never forgive me for what I did with you, nor it's an act that deserves forgiveness. All I want is just one change to improve my mistake, so that if we got successful in your rescue than I might forgive myself for this sin.

A river of tears started falling from her eyes, which filled the dearth ocean of Dushyant's eyes as well. Some more tears dropped from his eyes and to hide them he moved up and stood next to the window. Kavya kept crying sitting on the floor, further she told Dushyant, that she is a culprit for him and his family and if he wants to send me back humiliating me then I will go back quietly, but if you have ever truly loved me for a moment, then please give me a chance to correct all my mistakes.

Dushyant still stood silent on that window, and Kavya kept crying on the floor. Finally, I went up to him and place my hand over his shoulder and said; brother that was a bad phase, and every one phased the consequences for that including her. Now she wants to correct things and prove her parents wrong, please allow her to re-open your case, please say yes.

Dushyant: I loved you from the bottom of my heart from the very moment I saw you first time, though we have made some mistake and done some blunder with our life but that doesn't mean our love is not pure. I don't know whether I will be able to forgive you in the future or not, but if you want to do it just to forgive yourself, you can try for it!

Suddenly there was a light of positivity came in our eyes. Kavya wipes her tears, she opened a file with the application of re-opening his case and forwarded to him to sign it. Dushyant looked once towards me and he signed the application. I hugged him for his decision, and Kavya dropped some more tears of joy and then he went back with the police constable.

Inside I was so happy, thinking, I was the one helped him initially for her love, now again I make a move to reunite these true lovers. Some tears of joy spilled through my eyes.

Chapter 6
Justice

After a few signatures of Dushyant our petition was fully ready, next day we both went to thecourt and submitted our petition. Then next morning it was hot news for the local newspapers, which spreads like a fire in the jungle in Yaadavon Ki Dhani to Qutub Pur to my village as well. The news spreads like Salman Khan's Movie trailer, now everybody wants to watch their story.

After a few days of petition submission, one notice reached at Kavya's home as well. Her uncle and her parents have decided that they will not let Kavya win this case at any cost, as now it's a matter of the prestige of their family in the society.

After waiting for few days Kavya went to Indore to ask for support and suggestions from his senior fellow lawyers there.

It was a Friday evening, I also left from my BSNL office to my apartment, after a few minutes of the drive only I saw one white Scorpio interrupted me and stopped my car on the road. Before I could have understood anything 5 armed people with Hockey sticks, chains, and knives in the hand attacked me, one of them was Atul's spy. They broke the front glass of my car and dragged me out of the car and started hitting me with all the possible ways. I tried to resist and escape but one solid blow on my head from the back made me unconscious, and what happened afterward, I don't remember anything exactly.

When I got conscious, I found myself in a hospital bed with a glucose needle in my hand. I felt pain in my head, but I tried to wake up but one sweet nurse standing next to my bed stopped me to do so now. I have bandages over my head and hand along with lots of small bruises. Mom and Dad came to my bed along with Rohan my office colleague, Mom started crying seeing me in this condition in hospital. Rohan and the nurse helped me to sit on the bed, I asked my mom to please stop crying I am fine they are just small bruises, Ouch I irked due to a cramp on my hand.

Rohan asked for my wellbeing and briefed me about yesterday's incident. After the attack on me, I fell on the road unconscious and before they tried to kill me Rohan and some other passing by colleagues of my office shouted and gathered some crowd and they run away. He also called the PCR and given the number of that vehicle and other details to the police.

My Dad further told me they have visited your apartment too, they were asking about you and Kavya and they have beaten the security guards created a nuisance at your apartment. Now I got understand that Kavya's uncle and Randhir were behind this horrible crime,they want us to withdraw our petition from the court as they can't bear to lose their fake respect in front of society.

Mom and dad were so concerned for me about this incident, my mom was telling me everything was running so smooth in life, now why do you want a rivalry from those goons? For god sake, if something happens to you what we will do? You're my only child my son and she started crying. I consoled her, my dear mom I will be completely fine in a few days you just don't worry. Further, I told them Dushyant was innocent and serving jail for a false conviction, Kavya has left everything behind including her family to fight for justice and get him free from the jail and I will support her in this task.

My father interrupted in between and said; everybody in the village is laughing at us, why are you participating in this? You have not done any wrong in this. If something happens to you how we will live our life? I assured them back that nothing will happen to me, I will take precautions in the future now. They are just threatening us so that we take our petition back as they know inside that we are going to win this case. I can't helped Dushyant at the time of his conviction but not now, we will get my friend out of the jail.

The big doctor came to check me in between and saw my x-rays and wounds. Further, he adds nothing to worry about as such now you can take a discharge tomorrow and you have to continue the medicines at home for next 10 days.

My mom and dad got some relief after hearing this, I asked them to return to the village now I am fine and Rohan is there with me to help. But they are adamant to stay with me until I got fully fit & fine and till the time this court case is active, they wished to live with me in Jaipur only.

Around 8:00 pm in the night, I asked mom to leave with Rohan to my apartment and take some rest, my father stayed with me at the hospital. After a while door of my room opened and Kavya came in terrified and started crying seeing me like this near my bed.

Kavya: I am so sorry, Hemant this all happened because of me.

Hemant: Please don't cry, I am fine! It's just small bruises and scratches only, nothing to worry about.

Kavya: No Hemant, already one of my friends serving a term in the jail because of me, and now all this happens with you.

Hemant: Kavya Please! We lost from them earlier also due of our fear, but not this time. It's because of you I can face my friend and look into his eyes after so many years. Now I am not going to ruin this again,you're my inspiration to fight for truth, please don't get afraid of anyone.Together we will achieve success in this case and justice will be served.

Kavya: But if something happens to you I will not be able to forgive myself ever, you're the only one now, who is with me at this difficult time of my life.

Hemant: Don't worry nothing will happen to me,you just focus more on the case.

Kavya: Alright! But you please be watchful around and take care of yourself, I will file a complaint against those goons and ask for a police protection for you.

Dad interrupted and said something which I was not expecting from him, I thought that he will shout on Kavya for all this but he said; don't worry my Childs now we all are with you in this fight, they can't do any further wrong with you. Kavya turned to my dad and greeted him with a smile and said Namaste! Uncle, Thank you so much for your support and I am so sorry that you people are facing all this because of me. My dad said "No my child don't be sorry, you guys are so brave, you took this bold step to fight for justice and also changed my thought process to stand with the truth, We are so proud of you, my blessings are with you guys and I hope you will be successful in your mission for sure."

Those words of my dad have boosted our confidence a lot, now we are more firm to achieve our goal to free Duhsyant from jail.

Next day, all my reports came normal except X-ray of my left hand, it got a small fracture in the elbow, So with a plaster in the hand, I got discharged from the hospital and suggested one week's complete rest with medication. But with the care and delicious food of my mom, I felt good after 5 days rest only.

In the evening, Kavya came to my apartment with a good news. I saw a big smile on her face. She came and said the court has accepted our petition and we got our first court date on 13th July 2011. That's great, and I got a wave of confidence and positivity in my body. My mother put her hand on Kavya's head and blessed her that you are going to win this battle, my blessings are with you guys.

Kavya has not slept from the past two nights, she was so busy in her case study of Dushyant and preparing her arguments. Dushyant's case was a hot topic of the city, post the attack on me, that's why it was so difficult to Randhir and Atul's gang to attack again on any of us.

13th July 2011

Finally, the day has arrived, we reach the court at the opening time, though our hearing was scheduled at 10:30 am. I don't know about Kavya but I was a little nervous inside. In the courtyard, we met Kavya's family, Randhir, Atul, and Basant Singh are staring us with fierce eyes, but Kavya and I have the confidence of truth in our eyes. We crossed our way with them keeping our heads up. When we get inside we came to know that they hired the same old lawyer of this case Vinod Badgadi as there representative. He is a crook lawyer and master of establishing fake allegations for the sake of money. He is an expert in criminal law and had set free a lot of culprits with his knowledge of law, he knows what point needs to use in what situation. His big fatty belly was a symbol that he is a top level bribe-taker and a corrupt person. In the gallery of the court, he tried to threaten and demoralize Kavya with his taunts along with rubbing his big fat belly.

Bagadi: Well-done girl, so now after reading a few pages of law you came to compete me in the court? You mad girl. I will not spare you this time, I will make you suffer so much that you will not able fight anymore case.

Kavya: Already people don't want to see your face at all, you are so corrupt that even your family members also not take you seriously. I will see you in the court and after losing the case from a newcomer that too a girl you will not able to show your face to anyone.

Bagadi: (laughs sarcastically) You are a little child in front of me, that's why I am warning you to take back your petition, there is nothing in this case for you, otherwise!

Kavya: Otherwise What? I will beat you in this case or else I will change my name from Kavya Yadav!

Bagadi got a little shock, looking at her confidence, he just moved from there angrily. Today everybody was there in the court from Kavya's family except her mother,her mother was in support of Kavya now, and she was also facing the anger of rest of the family members. On the other side, Dushyant's family has very little hope from this case now, that's why after my persistence also they denied gently to be a part of this case now, as they don't want to take chances of more disgrace to their family.

Judge of this case Mrs. Mehta arrives in the court room, and everybody stood up, she sat on her chair, and finally, the procedure of the court begins. Kavya initiated the case with her points of petitions. Dushyant also came in the court and stand silent in the convict box.

Kavya: Honourable Ma'am, five years back my client Dushyant Thakur has been convicted for a 10-year jail term for a false rape case. Which was based on some hostile witnesses and tempered reports, he was trapped in this case because he was not having proof of his innocence. But here today, I will present my points to prove the innocence of my client and will try that he will get back to his normal life with his dignity. I have submitted my detailed report of my plea, I request you to please have a look on that.

Judge: Mr. Bagadi?

Bagadi: (Stood up, holding his falling belt from his big-fat belly) My lord, This young lady is a bit under experience as this is her first case, out of excitement she forgets that court doesn't declare judgments on the basis of feelings, the court acts on facts and proofs.

Kavya: Objection my lord, I suggest my fellow lawyer talk about Dushyant and case only, instead of my age and experience.

Judge: I suggest you Mr. Bagadi to focus on the case-related points only.

Bagadi: Sure my lord,this petition is wasting the precious time of the court, as this case file has nothing in it to defend that boy. He has committed a heinous crime of rape, and I did proved this fact already in the district court five years back. My client has testified her statement that she has been raped by that boy Dushyant you can ask her directly? (Pointing his hand towards Kavya).

Judge: Mr. Bagadi, I suggest you to please maintain the decorum of the court and you can ask questions from anyone but in the witness box only.

Bagadi: Yes My lord, Miss Kavya, can you please come in the witness box? I have some questions to ask from you to clear this case.

Judge: Permission granted.

(Kavya removed her black lawyer coat and moved in the witness box.)

Bagadi: 5 years back you have testified that Dushaynt has forcefully raped you in your father's fields? Yes or NO!

Kavya: My lord I was just a juvenile at that time and I was not mature enough to discriminate between right and wrong, I didn't knew what I should talk in a courtroom. Some of my family members have an old arch rivalry with Thakur family, and they have used me against them. Today I am wise enough to stand for the truth and fight for justice. I have misled the court under the threats and pressure of my family, I consider myself equally responsible for his conviction, and I am ready to serve any punishment for my deed, but I cannot live with this guilt, for the sin I have done, and I will fight to any extent to get him out of the jail. He is innocent my lord.

Bagadi: (laughing sarcastically) my lord, I have asked for a simple yes or no, Somebody please tell this young lady that it's not a children's puppet play, it's a court of law, here we work on evidence only, not on the guilt of your wrong deeds.

Kavya: My lord, I am aware of the importance of proofs and evidence in the court and very soon I will prove my client Dushyant an innocent, and the proofs are used to convict him, are false and tempered.

Bagadi: (laughing out loud) my lord, as far as I know, she is just wasting the precious time of the court and nothing else.

Kavya: My lord, the law will only see and hear what is presented in front of the court, my client was beaten so badly by these people (pointing towards Randhir, Atul & gang) that he was even not able to stand in the court properly. He and his family have not given sufficient time to defend his case. Today I asked you for that time so that I can prove it that Dushyant Thakur has not done any crime for which he was suffering in jail.

Bagadi: But my lord…

Judge: (Interrupting Bagadi) Ms. Kavya I hope that without wasting the court's time, you will bring out all the important points of this case in front of us, and Mr. Bagadi I suggest you to please co-operate with her and instead of your vague talks try to speed up the proceedings for a faster result. The next hearing of this case will be held on 22nd July 2011. (And judge ma'am moved out of the court room)

Bagadi was crushing his teeth's, while Kavya has a new ray of hope on her face. In the courtyard, she was discussing with me that we have to bring Dushyant's family to the court that will create extra support for us and Dushyant,but both of us have tried it, I told her. We must try one more time, she said and we made a plan to visit his family once again.

The next day at Dushyant's home his mom and dad denied talking to Kavya, they are still having grudge against her which is quite natural as well, but Kavya did one last request to Thakur Saab and said, "I know, I am a culprit of you all along with Dushyant, but trust me Dadu I assure you that if needed I will sacrifice everything, I have to win this case to bring Dushyant back to his home, If you people will also come and support me then it will give me strength and motivation to strive hard for my cause, please support me Dadu."

Thakur Saab: My child I know that my grandson is innocent, he just cannot do any crime, but you just cannot understand the amount of slander and profanity we people had gone through in last five years, going to the court means all those wounds of profanity will become fresh again, and we don't have the courage to bear all that once again.

Kavya: Dadu I can understand the suffering and pain you have gone through, but please come and join this fight for Dushyant, I know that you love him more than anything in this world, The next court date is on the 22nd of July, I request you to please come to the court for Dushyant, we will wait for you.

He didn't reply to this, but his eyes are saying that he does want to join us for Dushyant, We left from there hoping at least Thakur

Saab will join us in this fight.

22nd July 2011.

For a surprise, Thakur Saab was there in the court before us, and he gave us a thumbs up and blessed us to win this fight. Court's procedure has begun Post-Judge Mrs. Mehta's arrival.

Bagadi: My lord, as I spoke in last hearing, in this case, I will not waste much of your time and I will try to wrap it as fast as possible with solid piece of evidences, I request you, please allow me to present some of the key witnesses related to this case into the witness box.

Judge: Permission granted.

Bagadi: I would like to call Dr. Kulkarni in the witness box please.

(He called in the court by the attendant of the Judge Madam).

(5 years back, Dr. Kulkarni has made the medical check-up reports of Dushyant and Kavya.). Dr. Kulkarni came into the witness box and took the oath, to tell the truth in front of the court.

Bagadi: So Dr. Kulkarni as you have taken the wow to speak the truth in front of the honorable court, can you please tell us the truth about their medical check-up reports which you did 5 years back?

Dr. Kulkarni: Yes your honour, I did the medical check-up of 5 years back, when the victim was brought to me she was terrified and she was having blood spots around her thighs and vaginal area, and her hymen was broken, then I took a sperm sample from the victim, which was matched by the rapist sperm sample, As per the samples and final medical reports, it shows that the victim was raped by rapist Dushyant only.

Bagadi: Well explained Dr. Kulkarni, I must say you do your duty very vigilantly.

Judge: Any question from him, Ms. Kavya?

Kavya: No my lord (very stressed).

Bagadi: My lord, now I would like to call another important eye witness of this case sub-inspector Basant Singh.

Judge: Permission granted.

(He also did the same ritual to take an oath to speak the truth.)

Bagadi: Mr. Basant Singh, can you please elaborate on 29th December around 4:30 pm what all have you saw at the crime spot?

Basant Singh: My lord, we got a call from a local villager about that incident, and when I reached on the crime spot with my team the culprit has already performed his crime. Cloths of the girl were completely torn and are having a lot of blood spots on it. We caught the Rapist on the spot red-handed and arrested him, further we have sent both of them to the hospital for medical check-ups.

Bagadi: Did you have taken any statement of the victim Mr. Basant?

Basant Singh: Yes my lord, after the medical check-up in her consent girl has stated that she is been forcefully and against her will raped by Dushyant. She had signed her statement also, and we have already submitted a copy of the same in the court.

Bagadi: Thank you Mr. Basant, my lord this case is crystal clear now, like the water of Bisleri. Hence, it is proved that Dushyant Thakur has done heinous crime of rape with the victim and serving the jail for his evil deeds only,that's all my lord from my side.

Judge: Ms. Kavya Yadav would you like to ask any question to him?

Kavya: No questions Ma'am.

The situation a bit tense after Bagadi's witness in the court, Thakur Saab and I also worried now that how will Kavya come back in this case now.

Judge: In the hearing of this case till now, I have heard and noted down the points of the accused side,now I will ask the defence lawyer to bring some crux proofs of Dushyant's innocence. We will hear them on the next date, and I will declare the final verdict on the same day only,the next hearing date of this case will be 2nd august 2011.

I drive my car with silence throughout the way to home, but at home, I burst out on Kavya. "How will we win this case with your silence? This is our final chance if you have nothing to speak in the court then why did you boast those things in front of me that you will set out my friend free? If you will not able to bring any solid evidence in front of the judge, she will declare the case in favour of Bagadi again."

Kavya: Hemant how will I tell you, I got scared after seeing those people in front of my eyes, I still have those dark reflections in my mind of that bad day. I just couldn't speak in front of them, my uncle Basant torn my clothes to establish the evidence, he has also beaten me up in the police station so that it will look like a forceful rape. He took my signature on a plain paper and wrote the statement himself to present it in the court. I still have a haunting sound of slaps from Basant Singh, Randhir, and my father (and she cried a little.)

Hemant: Relax Kavya, this is the past only now please get over this as soon as possible, they cannot even touch you now. You have to stand in front of them, and you have to fight for justice,we have to win this case for Dushyant! (I hold her from both the hands and motivated her).

Kavya didn't reply to me and she just kept looking at my hopelessness for a minute and then she left for her room. She didn't talk much with me for 2 days and kept her in isolation. She was a bit tense due to the pressure of the final date of our case, I tried to discuss things over evening Chai with her, but she didn't speak much.

Next morning, when I woke up, I saw Kavya was not there at home. I asked my mom about her she said, she left the home early morning without saying anything, and even she didn't have breakfast also. She went to Kishan Garh Jail to meet Dushyant, perhaps she wants to discuss something important with him or she wants to raise some crucial points for which she requires his permission first.

After two days it will be the decisive day for us, I was very nervous and praying to the God for a positive result on the final day.

2nd August 2011.

Finally, the judgment day has come, today will be the last day of defence hearing in the court just after Mrs. Mehta will pass her final judgment on the case. Today also Kavya left from home early saying that she has some work, she was looking very nervous today, her behaviour sounded a bit strange to me and I was concerned about her. I reached court with my mother and father and we all were so tense about the result.

Today people's strength was a bit extra than usual because of the judgment day.Kavya was already there in the court busy with her case files. Judge Mrs. Mehta came in and court's procedure begun for the final day. Everybody was gazing at Kavya, will she able to prove Dushyant innocent today?Will she able to set him free? But in mind was one question was haunting me again and again that why Kavya was so quite from the last few days?

Judge: Ms. Kavya please begin the defence arguments.

Bagadi: (sarcastically) your honour, she had no argument left to prove, this case is very clear that the convict is rightfully serving the term for his heinous deed of rape, I suggest you just pass your judgment.

Kavya: Mr. Bagadi why are you so impatient, let me present my points then its court's job to decide who is a criminal and who is innocent. My lord, I need your permission to call Dr. Kulkarni in the witness box.

Judge: Permission granted.

Kavya: Dr. Kulkarni, have you ever seen me outside the court? (She just asked this abruptly for a quick response).

Dr. Kulkarni: Yes just two days before in the city hospital, apart from this I don't remember any event.

Kavya: Dr. Kulkarni, you might forget that 5 years back you only did my medical check-up and confirmed I wasraped.

Dr. Kulkarni: What? As far as I remember I haven't seen you before this court hearing.

Kavya: Please try to remember Dr. Kulkarni, as per court's medical report it was you who checked me up medically and confirmed in this report that I was being raped.

Dr. Kulkarni: Yes, this report is mine and prepared by me, but the victim was you that I cannot confirm.

There were whispers in the court room after that statement.

Judge patted her wooden hammer on her table and asked for order in the court.

Kavya: And may I know the reason why?

Dr. Kulkarni: Because I couldn't see the face of the victim at that time, it was covered with a shawl,and even when I tried to saw her face sub-inspector Basant Singh has stopped me to do so. So then I just checked up the body and did the medical check-up. The body was raped and when I asked about the name of the victim, Basant Singh only told me Kavya and I prepared the report by the name of Kavya.

Kavya: Point to be noted, My Lord! Five years back the body which was examined by Dr. Kulkarni was raped, but that victim was not me and only my name was used to prepare a false report. I can say this thing in the court with so much conviction because I have also seen Dr. Kulkarni in the court for the first time, and as far as that medical report is concerned that report was right but it was not my report my lord. I have not been raped that day by Dushyant, ma'am we didn't have any major physical touch that day which anyone can justify as a rape, and to prove that I have submitted a new report of Dr Kulkarni, which he made himself it after my whole body check-up. It is mentioned in the report that till date I have not made any physical intercourse with any man and my hymn is perfectly intact!

There was a lot of noise and whispers in the courtroom, after this strange proof of virginity presented by Kavya.

Judge: Order order! Silence, please!

Kavya: Your Honour, apart from Dr. Kulkarni I have also submitted my medical check-up report from a Senior Doctor of Sawai Maan Singh hospital Jaipur, that report also confirmed that I am still a virgin girl.

Bagadi: (Out of fear) Bullshit! What utter nonsense and cheapness you have spread in the court young girl.

Kavya: Shut up! Mr. Bagadi, Mind your language.

Judge: Mr. Bagadi, Please have control over your words before you speak it in the court room.

Kavya: Your honour, nothing had happened on that day between Dushyant and me. He is already suffering from the last five years in Jail for a crime that he did not committed. I will also admit that I had made a big mistake in my life at that time, and I am ready to serve any punishment for the same. Those people who have misused the law and tempered the evidence to convict an innocent for a false case of rape,those people who have used the law as their puppets should be punished for their crimes. That's all your honour! (And she breaks down in the court).

After a few minutes of silence in the court, Ms. Mehta reads her final judgment after verifying all her medical reports.

Judge: After going through all the points, witnesses, and proofs, the court is accepting that some points of this case are very crucial and truthful which are presented in the court by Ms. Kavya. Dushyant is innocent in this case, and whatever happened at that time between Kavya and Dushyant was established as raped based on false reports and misleading statements. This court is apologizing to Dushyant and his family on the behalf of law for the wrong verdict given by the district court five years back, and based on all medical reports and the witness's, I reject all the allegations that pointed on Mr. Dushyant and I pass this order to immediately release him from the Jail with all due respect and honour. Also, I order to crime branch to further investigate this case and identify all the real culprits of this case and file a formal charge sheet against them.

Ms. Kavya you also are given a wrong statement in the court at that time, which is not an excuse in the eyes of law but considering your juvenile age and pressure by your family, court has released a fine order to you for sum of the Rupees fifty thousand.

After the final verdict by honourable Judge Madam, she humbly asked Dushyant he can speak few words, if he would like to say something about his case. Immediately after that line everybody turns towards Dushyant, with lot of curiosity, as everybody wants to know about his feelings now.

On the other side Dushyant's deep moist eyes were sparkling with the glory of truth, after a long pause finally he stood up and broke his silence.

Dushyant: Last 5 years of my life in the jail was so dark and painful, there was so much loneliness that I had given up on all the hopes to get back a normal life. These five years had passed like a long span of fifty years for me, it was so stressful to pass every single day in that cage. I always kept thinking about what is the purpose of my life now? But somewhere at the bottom of my heart, I always wished to tell my Dadu, my mother, my father and Kavya that what I have done with her was wrong but I am not a rapist.

All the eyes were moist at that moment in the court, Kavya can't controlled her emotions and tears, and she just kept on gazing at his face.

Dushyant: At that time I was not able to differentiate between what is more wrong, that decision of the court, or my act with Kavya, or I was just passing through the worst phase of my life. I was not even sure about the punishment of the court which I got was right or wrong, may be this was my destiny. But I deserve a punishment for myself for breaking your trust and faith in me, I deserve a punishment for crossing my limit that day, I deserve a punishment for vilifying the prestige of my family.

Though court has set me free from all the allegations now but I am your culprit Kavya, please forgive me for every wrong thing that I had done with you, please forgive me! (with folded hands he looked towards Kavya and she started crying.)

I don't know how I can thank you more for returning me my home, my village and my friends. You have given my life back, now I want to go home and tell everyone that perhaps what I did was wrong but I am not a rapist. Kavya I want to hug you so tight and tell you that I still love you more than anything else in my life. I still love you the same way when I saw you first time and fell in love with you. (and they kept looking at each other with tears in their eyes).

There was pin drop silence in the court on this, after a pause Judge Madam removed her glasses from her moist eyes and she stood up applauding for them, following her footsteps everybody stood up in the court room and started applauding. Everybody wants to meet Dushyant and Kavya to congratulate them on the victory of truth.

Finally, the truth has won over the lie, everybody rushed to Kavya to congratulate for her first victory as a lawyer, everyone was praising her for the courage she has shown in this case and gone against all odds and highlights such a sensitive point as a piece of evidence that too being a girl.

Thakur Saab and I reached to her, and he performed a Salute with full pride in front of her and kissed her forehead for fighting for the truth and saving the rest of the life of Dushyant, and with the tears of joy in my eyes I hugged Kavya tightly, we cried a little more and I said "You did it Kavya, You have won the case Kavya", she interrupted and said "No without your support it won't be possible for me to win this case", and she corrected me and said "We won the case".

On the other side, Dushyant was still standing silent, though finally, it has proven in the court that he is not guilty. Kavya and I rushed to him and hugged each other,It was truly the best possible happy reunion for us though it was tough and much delayed. Thakur Saab also joined us in between and finally, long-awaited happiness was around us.

Randhir, Basant Singh, Atul, and Kavya's other family members left the room with their neck's down. Bagadi came to Kavya and gave a formal congratulation and said "You fought well,you will be a big lawyer soon, all the best and he also left the room".

Everybody wants to see Kavya and Dushyant, finally, Dushyant was released from the cuffs and we came together out of the court with a smile.

Chapter 7
Reunion

The news of this verdict reached the entire area, before we reached the village. Dushyant's family was waiting curiously for us to arrive at home. Just after reaching at home his mother rushed and hugged him, his father also joined them.

After all, it was proven with the facts that Dushyant was not a rapist, seeing his mom and father after five years the sea of tears came out from the eyes of Dushyant,but these are tears of joy, everybody was so much into the joy of tears that no one could describe their fillings at that time with anyone. His father Thakur Pratap Singh couldn't believe in his eyes that finally, his son came back home with the same pride and honour as before. It felt to them like the light of hope has come back to their dark lives. Her mother welcomed him back with traditional Aarti and Tilak. In all this hustle-bustle Kavya left from there silently.

After a while when I felt her absence, I started looking for her, but she was not there. Dushyant and all his family members asked about her, but she was already left there.

I tried her phone several times, but it was showing switched off, her leaving us like this without saying a word has shocked us all. We all got concerned for her, we also searched for her, all around but all in vain. Whole night Dushyant and I could not sleep because of her leaving us like that.

Nextmorning we came to know that she left the town after meeting her mom yesterday, as Yadav family has already disowned her, but she even didn't tell her mother that where was she going.

Few days have passed, Thakur Saab and his whole family got concerned for her as somebody might do wrong with her after this verdict, Dushyant and I also got so concerned for her after all this.

Then one evening I got a call from Dushyant that bro please

be ready tomorrow morning, we are going to Udaipur tomorrow for some urgent work by early morning 5:00 am express train,I will meet you at the Rewari station at 4:30 am. I got a little surprised on this that why suddenly Dushyant want to go to Udaipur? Anyway the next day early morning one of my friend dropped me at the Rewari railway station, the train was also on time that day,around at 4:40 pm, we reached Udaipur junction, and we went out of the station. Dushyant asked one auto driver to go to Fateh Sagar Lake, the auto driver agreed and we boarded that auto. Here on the other side, I was amazed that he said we have an important work here, now he wants to roam around the lake in the evening.

Anyway, we reached at the lakeit was a pleasant evening and the sky was a bit cloudy as it was about to rain. August was usually a rainy season here in Udaipur and this is the best time of the year to visit here. It was bit crowded here and I got a feeling that we might came here for evening walk and snacks only, but Dushyant was silently looking for someone as if he is searching for something precious. Besides the lake, there is a big footpath on which people are sitting and enjoying the views, I was just walking behind Dushyant, but he was constantly looking for someone in the crowd. Suddenly the rain has started, some people ran to save themselves from getting wet, while some are enjoying the rain. I got my new phone in my hand for which I was concerned, I called Dushyant let's to go back and take a shelter but he didn't listened to my voice perhaps because the sound of the rain, he just didn't want to stop at that point. So I have no option but just to follow him, after a while, Dushyant has stopped, and we saw a girl standing under a small dome and feeling drops of rain with her hands. Dushyant speaks, Kavya! And she turned towards us, I got a surprise that it was she. It reminded me the same moment of our school time, when it was raining, and we saw her first time feeling the rain with her hands. But before I could understand anything Dushaynt goes closer to the dome and both looked at each other and cried.

Dushyant: I knew it! You will be here only, why did you left us, without saying anything?

Kavya: Why? Did you come here Dushyant.

Dushyant: You have given me this new life, and I want to live it with you only,don't you give me a chance to live my life again?

Kavya: No Dushyant, I don't want to go back there, I have nothing left there.

Dushyant: Seriously? Your childhood friends, your love,everybody is missing you there. Just look at me, you saved my life to correct your mistake, Now, won't you give me a chance to correct mine?

Kavya started gazing at him with wet and numb eyes.

Dushyant: We have wasted so many years without each other, but now I couldn't live without you for a moment. My childhood friend Kavi is missing somewhere, can you please give me back my Kavi? Will you give the love of my life back to me? Please!

Hearing this, she smiled while tears are kept dropping from her eyes. Fast lighting struck with a massive thunder sound and she hugged him tightly under the dome and rain further intensified. I was watching this from just a few feet away and I just couldn't express my joy at that time. After a minute they wiped each other tears and Dushyant looked towards me and said "Why are you standing far bro?" And I rushed to them and hugged my best friends.

The next day, Whole Thakur family came to Udaipur along with Kavya's Mother to give the new couple their blessings.

Present-day August 2019.

I am going to Udaipur, *Deewano Se Milne*(meet the lovers). Today also I think that who these people are,thoughthey are also from this mean world, but yet they are so different from this world.

Anyway, on their wedding anniversary, I am taking a special gift for them,the first copy of my first book, their love story "NOT A RAPIST".

The End.